Camille kissed her shoulder and slowly worked her way down to a breast, licking and sucking gently as Nicole's fingers toyed with her thick brown hair. It had been months since Camille had endured such bliss. She kissed the softness of Nicole's stomach and eventually reveled in the taste of her. She gently probed with her tongue, remembering having wanted to do this the first night they had met.

"Oh, yes . . . ," Nicole murmured as she clutched the corners of her pillow with one hand, while burying the other in Camille's hair. "Yes . . ." Her voice trailed off and her breathing quickened.

LOVE'S HARVEST

PEGGY HERRING

THE NAIAD PRESS, INC.
1996

Printed in the United States of America on acid-free paper
First Edition

Editor: Lisa Epson
Cover designer: Bonnie Liss (Phoenix Graphics)
Typesetter: Sandi Stancil

Library of Congress Cataloging-in-Publication Data

Herring, Peggy J., 1953—
    Love's Harvest / by Peggy Herring.
        p.   cm.
    ISBN 1-56280-117-1
    1. Wine and wine making—France—Fiction.   2. Lesbians—
France—Fiction.   I. Title.
PS3558.E7548L68   1995
813'.54—dc20   95-39245
                                                                      CIP

For Frankie

About the Author

Peggy J. Herring is a 1953 baby who was raised on rock 'n roll, moon pies and "I Love Lucy." She lives on seven acres in South Texas with her lover of twenty years and their two cockatiels. When she isn't writing, Peggy enjoys fishing, camping and traveling.

Chapter One

The winery buzzed with activity as the first group of tourists arrived. Nicole was glad that Antoine had offered to take them; his English was getting better with each bus that stopped in the parking lot. She watched him gather the tourists in close like a shepherd tending a new flock. He gave them each a colorful brochure and made them laugh easily as they began asking him questions. Nicole left him, confident that he would be both entertaining and informative, and made her way down the short hallway to the nursery. She would finally have a little time to herself.

Nicole Jeton enjoyed everything about being a winemaster — from deciding when a particular vintage was ready to be sold to inspecting and cleaning the equipment they used for the harvest. Very little went on that she wasn't involved in. She worked with each employee individually several times during the day. No job was too small; she had done them all at one time or another. The nursery, however, would always hold a special place in her heart, and just being among the small plants in their most delicate stages soothed her completely.

Her love for the vineyards had started here when she was a child. Every April she had helped her father with the young grafts that would someday replace old or damaged vines in the vineyards. Nicole remembered how Papa had cared for the sprigs and how eager she had been to help whenever he needed something. She smiled as she gently touched a tender new leaf from an already established shoot. This had also been her father's favorite part of the winery.

Nicole reached for the old watering can and was momentarily amazed at how much lighter it had gotten over the years. Every morning as she tended to the new plants she thought of her father. His patience with her eagerness had been a blessing, something she would always remember.

"More water, Papa? Don't they need more water?" she would ask him.

Even now Nicole could remember his deep laughter as he nodded his graying head. "Just a little, I think," he would say before helping her with the watering can. Nicole always felt very close to him in the nursery. He had taught her well.

At college she had been a chemistry major, her vast knowledge of winemaking apparent even as a teenager. In school Nicole took classes with future physicists, chemists, and doctors, who all laughed when she told them she would be a winemaster someday. "No one goes to college for that," they had said. "You have such a bright future in medicine! Why settle for so menial a profession?" Nicole was the first person in her family to go to college. Chemistry and physics she had learned there, but winemaking she had learned from her father.

The people at the winery prepared for the harvest all year long. As a little girl Nicole had been everywhere begging to help. At the blessing of the vineyards each fall, a ritual that they hoped ensured a profitable crop, Nicole remembered holding Papa's big rough hand as the priest in his habit flung holy water and recited a prayer in heavily accented French. It had always been her favorite part of the harvest. From there the activity was nonstop.

After the crop was finally in, Papa would get a crate for Nicole and her brother, Lalo, to stand on so they could help crush the grapes in a large wooden vat. They each had their own wooden paddles and were always so careful as they stirred. Lalo bored easily and was off playing elsewhere before long, but Nicole stayed and tended to the grapes, feeling as though each and every one belonged only to her.

She tagged along behind her father, month after month, year after year, learning more than anyone thought possible for someone so young. It was

3

assumed that Lalo would eventually carry on the family tradition of winemaking, but he had discovered his passion for young men and had more important things to do. The moment winemaking became work, Lalo had lost all interest in it. He had no intention of ever having to go to work if at all possible.

Nicole remembered how cold and quiet the winters had seemed at the winery when she was a child. January brought with it a time for relaxation for them, with the ground frozen and the vines dormant. Nicole spent time with Papa in the lab then, sitting on a stool next to his, watching as he held test tubes up to the light. This had undoubtedly sparked her first interest in chemistry.

Nicole set the watering can down and took off her gloves. She stretched the kinks out of her back and glanced around the nursery. Everything was always in its place. She liked that. A Jeton Vineyards calendar hung on a rusty nail near the door. Nicole scanned it and smiled. She ordered new calendars every year with the same picture of the château at the top. It was just one of many traditions she had chosen to continue. She liked consistency, liked knowing what was expected of her every morning when she woke up. The life of a winemaster seldom changed, with certain things done at certain times. Nicole studied the calendar further and scanned the months with interest.

In February they pruned. It was cold and bitter, not anyone's favorite month at the winery. As a child, Nicole hadn't been permitted to observe the pruning process until she was much older, even though she begged to go to the vineyards with her father every day from the time she was five. The weather was too harsh for one so young, and Nicole had never been a patient child. Now she thought back on those times fondly while she and Antoine were out there in the vineyards with the others. Nicole supervised and shivered right along with everyone else. At times it could be miserable work, but she loved it. They all loved it.

March and April were much more reasonable months, with more pruning before the vines woke up and the shoots began to run. The nursery became active then, with new grafts being laid in damp sawdust or sand and kept at controlled temperatures. Nicole tended to each graft carefully, lovingly, as if every sprig were a link to the future.

In May there was always the threat of frost. She could remember Papa going to the vineyards every morning, checking and recording anything significant. Even now Nicole rode out to the vineyards bright and early on mornings in May, sometimes thinking of him as she scribbled in her notebook. As a teenager she had learned the importance of logging everything concerning the crop and the harvest. All pesticides and weed killers, their uses and effects, were recorded and used for future reference. Unusual weather was recorded: droughts, floods, out-of-season cold snaps. Everything. She had watched her father do this day after day and eventually was allowed to help him with it. The paperwork at times was overwhelming.

June, however, was always the tricky month. It usually brought calm, warm weather when the vines began to flower. The absence of severe rain and wind was critical at this point. Nicole always watched the weather as closely as she watched the vines. Luck was just as important a factor as skill in this business.

"Too much rain," she remembered her father saying one morning in mid-June the summer before she went away to college. Their horses followed along behind them as they looked down at the vineyards from the ridge. "Rain in June is good, Nicole. But not so much. It has to stop soon." And stop it did. The weather had given them several scares over the years, but never anything they couldn't recover from.

July was a more leisurely time for them, the nursery being the main concern while the grapes in the vineyards flourished. Nicole had stayed close to the lab whenever Papa was there and she was not in school. He would pour a small sample of wine in a glass and hold it up to the light. Seeing him take the glass carefully in his big hands always made her smile as he swirled, sniffed, and then sipped the glass's contents. He would purse his lips playfully and make a little smacking noise that always made her laugh.

"Taste this, Nicole. See how sweet?"

Nicole would take the glass from him and swirl and smell its remaining contents before tasting any of it. "Yes, Papa."

"Coming along nicely. Much different from last time?" he would ask as he jotted down notes.

"Much different," she agreed. "Less acid."

He would smile then, having very little idea what sort of chemical changes took place during the fermentation process. He only knew when the time was right.

Nicole was now the winemaster, and she spent

hours tasting and testing the various vintages. Her father had been seriously ill for several years now, and seemed to be getting even worse these last few months. Nicole's credibility as his successor, however, had never been questioned. The wine industry had accepted her immediately. Nicole's flair for business and her vast knowledge of wine was evident in everything she did. She had earned the respect of those who knew of such things. Under her management, the winery's profits were higher than they had ever been since her grandfather's death fifty years ago. Several good crops and shrewd negotiations with buyers helped the financial security of the Jeton family.

Nicole heard Antoine's baritone voice carry from the vat room over to the nursery. She knew how fortunate she was to have him. Good cellarmasters did not come along easily. She and Antoine enjoyed riding down to the vineyards together, seeing the grapes along the landscape amid several flashes of pink and green. They worked closely together during the year and prepared for the harvest every day. The harvest was everything; the excitement always kept spirits high. The winery would be humming with activity as baskets, crushers, hods, vats, pipes, destalkers, and presses were cleaned and inspected. Nicole had to keep an even closer eye on the weather during this time. Because too much rain could ruin the crop, there was an ever-present desire among most of the staff to harvest early. Antoine and Nicole always checked the vineyards together daily when they were close to harvesting.

"They're ready," Antoine had said the year before. He looked at the sky nervously and then back at the grapes. "I say we harvest tomorrow. I'll talk to the priest."

"Let's wait. It won't rain."

Antoine threw his hands up in the air, exasperated. Year after year she was willing to take a chance, while the waiting made Antoine so nervous that he couldn't sleep at night. The longer they held off on the harvest, the better and sweeter the grapes would be. Antoine, being the pessimist that he was, had nightmares of hailstorms or weeks of rain that would either destroy the crop or make the harvest impossible. Nicole, however, was the winemaster, and the decision when to harvest was hers and hers alone. So far she had always been right.

She checked the temperature in the nursery and made a few adjustments before going upstairs to her office to finish some paperwork. The sale of a particular vintage was within days of closing, and she wanted everything ready when the time came. A while later she heard the chattering of tourists from the parking lot as they boarded their bus. Nicole glanced at her watch. She wanted to spend some time with her father before lunch.

Chapter Two

Camille raced down the hall, her long skirt swooshing as she went. She reached the elevator only seconds before its doors closed behind her. Rearranging the folders in her arms and setting her briefcase down, she checked her watch. Late again. *You have to start leaving the apartment earlier,* she reminded herself. Every morning she was up in plenty of time, but things just never seemed to go as planned.

The moment the elevator door dinged open again, Camille rushed out. She burst into her office and glanced at the clock on the wall, hoping that possibly her watch had been wrong. A stack of telephone messages was handed to her on the way by.

"Your cousin has called three times already," Adel said. "And the editor wants to see you."

Camille went into her office and dropped the folders and the messages on her already cluttered desk. *The editor,* she thought. *Not good.* She selected several folders from the stack and handed them over to her secretary. "Any idea what he wants?"

Adel shook her head.

"Send these back," Camille said, indicating the folders. "Call and tell him I'm on my way."

She hurried out of her office and back down the crowded hallway, oblivious to the overt glances meant only for her. With her head held high and shoulder-length dark hair bouncing with each step, she braced herself for a lecture on punctuality. The boss could be a stickler about such things. He hadn't so much as spoken to her in three months.

"Good morning," Camille said pleasantly to the editor's assistant. "He's expecting me."

The woman looked up and smiled. "Good morning, Mademoiselle Cartier. Yes, he's been waiting for you. Go on in."

Not good, Camille thought again as she smoothed her skirt and stepped into his simple but tastefully decorated office.

"Ah, Camille," he said brightly, and rose from his chair. "Come in."

"Good morning. You wanted to see me?" She was surprised at the calm in her voice. This was not one of her favorite people. He motioned for her to sit down.

"I just wanted to congratulate you on the way you've turned your department around," he said. Even though he was several inches shorter than she, the chair behind his desk gave one the impression that he was much taller. Camille often wondered if his feet touched the floor when he sat down. "In the six months since you transferred," he continued, "you've managed to clear out most of the backlog, and I've heard nothing but good reports in your dealings with the other sections."

Camille was nearly speechless as she stared at him. Compliments? He was giving her compliments? She hadn't expected this.

Back in her own office she was once again bombarded with telephone messages. "Your cousin called again," Adel informed her as she waved the message in the air.

Camille pulled the slip of paper from the stack and dialed Marguerite's number, wondering what national emergency had arisen since they had last spoken the night before.

"Marguerite," Camille said, getting comfortable behind her desk, "four messages before eight-thirty? Are you all right? Is someone ill?"

"Camille," Marguerite oozed, "you were so evasive when we spoke last. Are you or are you not coming to our party tonight?"

Camille took a deep breath, sighing heavily. She thought she had made her position quite clear already. She hated Marguerite's parties. They were nothing more than elaborate, boring business meetings for Marguerite's husband and his male clients. In addition to that, Marguerite was forever trying to fix her up with the most eligible of the

11

eligibles, even though Camille had made it quite clear that she was a lesbian and had no interest in any of it. Marguerite, however, never gave up trying, and Camille sometimes wondered if perhaps she herself was to blame for this continued persistence. Maybe she had somehow failed to make her position absolutely clear.

"I have work to do this evening," Camille said lamely.

"Work, work. You work too hard. Play is good too."

Camille laughed. "You give me nothing to play with, Marguerite. Your parties are boring."

"Boring?"

"Boring. String quartets. Tiny crustless sandwiches. Men. Boring, Marguerite. Positively boring."

"The entertainment and the food I can do something about, dearest," Marguerite said dryly, "but our guests are always the same. They ask for you when you're not here. Each says it hurts his business when you don't show up. Please come. For me. Please." Marguerite paused for a moment. "A jazz ensemble? Crepes?"

"Women?" Camille added in the same tone of voice her cousin had used. She chuckled and then sighed again. "What time?"

After she hung up, she was absolutely amazed at Marguerite's ability to get her way. *I'm much too available,* Camille thought with a smile. It never once occurred to her to lie to her cousin, feigning plans that she really didn't have. Eventually something interesting was bound to happen at one of those quaint gatherings, she reminded herself.

By late that afternoon Camille had her desk seemingly uncluttered and a briefcase full of manuscripts eagerly awaiting her attention. During the drive home she mulled over what she would wear to Marguerite's party and decided against catching a nap before getting ready. A few cleverly placed yawns after an hour or two would work in her favor as far as leaving early was concerned.

She put the finishing touches on her makeup and eyed herself critically in the mirror. She thought she had spotted a few wrinkles around her eyes earlier. Camille looked more closely and tossed her wavy, shoulder-length dark hair. At thirty-five she didn't feel as though she deserved wrinkles yet. *It's these awful hours I keep,* she thought wearily.

She arrived at Marguerite's shortly after eight. One glance across the enormous room filled with suited men told her this was no different than any of the other events she had attended here.

Marguerite spied her and came gliding over, wasting no time before launching into a conversation with three balding eligibles. Camille, having been properly trained in the social graces of Parisian high society, automatically smiled at the right time and laughed on cue at whatever was said. One man in particular kept rubbing his elbow against her arm each time someone laughed. Marguerite had introduced him as someone in electronics. Camille was aware that he kept standing at an odd angle to her, and she finally realized he knew she was tall enough to see his bald spot easily. The other two men were much older, but age didn't lessen the attention they focused on her. One of them had made millions in the import business, while the other was involved in the music industry. If the conversation dragged even for a moment, Marguerite was right there to revive it.

A string quartet in the other room was virtually ignored by everyone. People continued to pour into the already crowded room. Camille managed to snatch a glass of champagne as the tray whizzed past her, and wondered briefly if there was anything to eat. She was starving. As the men slipped into a conversation on world economics, Camille sipped her champagne and went to search for an hors d'oeuvre or two.

Marguerite finally located her at the buffet table. "Here you are. I should have known where I'd find you."

"No crepes? No jazz?" Camille said as she took a tiny bite of a triangular-shaped sandwich. "You promised to do better, Marguerite. You got me here under false pretenses again."

"I didn't have time to phone the caterer, and all the jazz ensembles in Paris are booked solid for two months."

Camille sipped her champagne and leaned closer to her cousin to whisper, "I'm leaving, and I won't be back until you have better music and real food."

Marguerite's boisterous laughter caught everyone's attention. "Don't be ridiculous." She lowered her voice conspiratorially and whispered in return, "Promising that you'll be here is the only reason some of these old fools come to these things. You're wonderful window dressing, my dear. I could make a fortune just selling your telephone number."

"Flattery doesn't work with me, Marguerite. You know that. Window dressing is no reason for me to give up a perfectly dull evening at home. There are women who do this for a living, you know. Get one of them next time." Camille set her empty glass down on a small table and looked toward the door to see how difficult it would be to get there.

"Now I suppose you'll be trying to convince me that you have something better to do with your time," Marguerite said.

"I'd rather be in traction than spend another minute here with your drooling, overdressed salesmen. Traction, Marguerite. Broken legs and everything."

"You never go anywhere or do anything," Marguerite said, ignoring her. "All you do is work. At least I'm getting you out and away from that."

Camille let her cousin help her with her coat. "This makes work seem so simple and alluring."

"The one in shipping has asked about you several times," Marguerite whispered. "I never know what to tell him."

Camille smiled and squeezed her cousin's hand. "Tell him I prefer women, and then ask him if he has a sister who might be interested. Tell him whatever you like. I don't really care what you tell him."

Marguerite eyed her menacingly for a moment and then shook her head. "I'm sure I can think of something to tell him."

Chapter Three

Nicole took the tray from the maid and set it carefully near her father's bed. He was awake, but listless. It had been weeks since he had been able to sit up alone. His dark brown eyes flickered recognition whenever he saw her, but still he couldn't speak. Nicole fed him slowly and told him the news from the winery. The doctors said that he had become feeble and didn't understand anything, but Nicole refused to believe it and talked to him as much now as she ever had.

"Would you like a shave, Papa? I can have Antoine help me."

Eating what little Nicole had been able to feed him had thoroughly exhausted him. He dozed briefly and then fell into a deep sleep. Nicole covered him against the sudden chill in the room. It had been several days since Nicole had felt Eva's presence there. The apparition of her long-dead ancestor brought little more than mild recognition from the household any more. Eva's presence in the château was accepted by everyone connected with the Jeton family. The servants carried on their duties as easily with as without Eva's being there. Occasionally the apparition was even welcomed.

"He'll be fine, Eva," Nicole said reassuringly. She fussed with the covers on the bed. "He'll be fine."

She left him in the care of his nurse and went to the library on the first floor of the château. Claudette, the downstairs maid, brought the stack of mail and Nicole's afternoon tea.

"We should both be here for dinner," Nicole said absentmindedly.

"Yes, Mademoiselle."

Nicole separated two envelopes from the stack. She opened Marguerite's letter first. It had been several months since she had heard from her. The envelope contained an invitation to dinner the next time Nicole was in town. Business sent Nicole to Paris several times a year, but Marguerite and her husband were just as busy as Nicole was. The three of them had managed only a brief visit the last time Nicole had gone to Paris. And now with her father still so ill, it would be next to impossible for Nicole to stay away from the winery for any length of time.

She tapped the corner of Marguerite's invitation against her cheek thoughtfully. They had been friends in college and had kept in touch over the years. She filed the dinner offer away in the back of her mind as she scanned the rest of the mail. A notice from a buyer with an even larger bid for the winery's six-year-old vintage at last made her smile.

Camille had managed to make it to work on time several days in a row. She noticed how her secretary seemed to grow even more amazed each morning that the phenomenon occurred. Camille's cousin, Marguerite, had a few comments as well.

"You're never there early, dear," Marguerite said when Adel put her through the first time. "I'm not sure I'm ready to talk to you yet."

"If it's about one of your —"

"Oh, yes," Marguerite said. "I remember now. Tomorrow. I have a surprise for you."

"No party," Camille said firmly. "I'm not interested."

"Of course it's a party. Entertaining is how we make money, dear. You won't have to stay long. Just make an appearance. In and out. The usual."

Camille could hear her cousin's bracelets jingling on the other end of the telephone.

"I've booked the entertainment you suggested," Marguerite continued. "And we're having crepes, Swedish meatballs, and some sort of quiche extravaganza. Real food, as you requested."

"I'm sure I have plans already," Camille said dryly. Cheesy pastries and a woodwind quartet were hardly reason enough to give up a perfectly dreary Thursday evening. She did, however, still owe her cousin a favor or two for helping her land an interview with one of Marguerite's husband's clients, but it was time to call it even. Getting herself in this position with Marguerite in the first place had not been a wise move on Camille's part, but at the time it had seemed like a good idea.

"This has to be the last one for a while. I have a life, Marguerite. As uneventful as you may think it is, I enjoy it just the same."

"Thank you. Thank you. Thursday at seven."

Camille arrived at her usual eight-fifteenish time and mingled with the crowd and sampled a few of the new treats Marguerite had arranged. Most of the faces Camille had seen before. Some were as regular as Marguerite herself.

"I can't say that the music is any better," Marguerite commented. "I've never quite understood the purpose of jazz. I can't hum to it. I can't dance to it. Why bother?"

The men who were clustered around them laughed delightedly. Empty champagne glasses were exchanged for full ones that the black-suited waiter offered. The little balding man who had been previously infatuated with Camille's elbow was there beside her again. She had dodged him quite effectively most of the evening.

"I have a surprise for you later," Marguerite whispered to her. Just then several heads turned toward the door, and the men around them seemed to hold their breath as they watched a woman slowly move into the room. She wore a dark blue dress and had auburn hair that reached past her shoulders. She removed her coat and glanced around uncertainly. The music stopped for a moment as the band moved into another song. Camille eyed her appreciatively along with the men but hoped she wasn't quite so obvious.

"Who is that exquisite woman?" someone beside them murmured.

Camille leaned closer to her cousin and whispered, "I hope that's my surprise."

"Nicole!" Marguerite squealed. "You were able to get away after all!" The two women embraced briefly while Marguerite scooped up a glass of champagne from a passing tray and placed it in Nicole's hand. "I had given you up. It's so late!"

"I was delayed, unfortunately. I'm sorry." The voice was like velvet in its softness. Camille realized she was staring along with everyone else but couldn't quite stop herself. *Make her speak again,* she secretly commanded.

"You work too hard. Play is good, too," Marguerite said with a light laugh.

Camille chuckled, having thought that line had only been reserved for her.

"Let me introduce you," Marguerite said with obvious pride as she led the woman farther into the room. "Everyone, this is Nicole Jeton."

Each man took Nicole's hand in turn and smiled dreamily. Had tails and tongues been capable of wagging, they certainly would have.

"And this is my dearest friend, Camille Cartier," Marguerite said finally.

Nicole smiled and nodded. Camille noticed she had that look a person gets after having been introduced to several people at the same time. Polite confusion registered vaguely. Their eyes met, and Camille found herself smiling easily as Nicole's gaze casually took her in.

"Nicole owns the Jeton Vineyards. She's the winemaster," Marguerite informed everyone proudly.

One of the men worked his way next to Nicole and expertly steered the conversation to wine, trying to dominate her attention. Nicole was polite and informative, but Camille noticed a slight tone of indifference in her answers to his persistent questions. She also noticed how Nicole waved her glass of champagne under her nose without taking a drink. She held the glass carefully but never tasted its contents.

Even though flashing smiles were still reserved for the new arrival, the men's conversation soon drifted back to business matters. Camille was relieved not to be the center of their attention any longer.

"*Camille,* is it?" Nicole asked politely after a while.

"Yes." Camille was surprised that she remembered her name. She found herself at a loss for words for a moment. Nicole's obvious uneasiness, however, spurred her on to make conversation. "I absolutely hate parties," Camille said.

"So do I," Nicole replied. "I've never had any time for social gatherings. Have you known Marguerite long?" Camille noticed how Nicole's glance kept stealing across the room to the door.

"Actually, we're cousins," Camille said with a laugh, "but she never seems to remember that."

Watching the young woman before her, Camille felt the minglings of excitement. She was drawn to her in a way that demanded her attention. *This is so much nicer than having one's elbow rubbed,* she thought. "How long have you known Marguerite?" Camille asked.

Nicole deftly placed her untouched glass of champagne back on a passing tray of drinks. "We were in college together." Nicole smiled shyly at Camille's astonished look. "Along with parties," she explained, "I also hate bad champagne."

Her comment seemed to pique an interest in the subject from the gentlemen there with them. Inquiries began pouring in on what in particular made a certain type of champagne good or bad. Nicole explained that she had been speaking of a preference instead of an actual scientific fact. Camille was amused at her ability to discourage their attention without offending them.

Nicole smiled shyly at her again and then inadvertently became drawn into another conversation with the small group.

"Are one of these yours?" Nicole whispered to Camille a few minutes later as she nodded toward the gentlemen next to them.

"One of what?"

Nicole waved her hand in the direction of the three men who were once again engrossed in the world of business. Camille laughed.

"Goodness, no," she said. "I'm here alone." Camille took a sip of her champagne. The alcohol on an empty stomach had caused her head to begin to swim a little. She suddenly leaned closer to Nicole and asked, "Would you join me on the veranda? It's much too noisy in here."

"Yes," Nicole said, her blue eyes sparkling.

Marguerite, however, caught them before they got very far. She took Nicole's arm and led her around and introduced her to several other people. Camille continued watching her and liked the way Nicole tossed her head back ever so slightly when she laughed. The moment Marguerite was called away on a problem in the kitchen, Nicole purposely set out to find Camille again. She scanned the crowd and then smiled the moment she saw her.

"We were on our way to the veranda," Nicole said.

Camille pushed the doors open and immediately appreciated the quiet. It was chilly out, but much nicer than where they had come from.

"How long will you be here?" Camille asked.

Nicole glanced at her watch. "I have to catch a train in a little while." She offered another shy smile. "I always take the train. I hate driving in the city."

Camille leaned against the railing that led out into the courtyard. "You hate parties, you hate bad champagne, and you hate driving in the city." Camille set her glass down on the railing. "Is there anything that pleases you?"

Those incredible blue eyes were suddenly curious and playful. Camille knew immediately that she and Nicole had several things in common, but she wasn't quite sure how to pursue the matter any further at the moment. There was always the chance that she might be wrong.

"I'm sorry," Nicole said. "Was I complaining?"

"No. Not at all." *Her eyes are the color of a summer sky,* Camille thought. *She's beautiful.* Pushing that thought away quickly, she said, "I can't remember Marguerite ever mentioning you before. Where are the Jeton Vineyards located?"

"In Burgundy. Just outside of Dijon. Over an hour's drive south."

"I know nothing about wine," Camille confessed. "I read somewhere that white goes with fish. Or is it red?" Camille dismissed the question with a wave of her hand. "All I really know is that I like most of it."

Nicole threw her head back and laughed. "You're priceless," she said. Their eyes met again briefly. "Are you married?" Nicole asked.

"No. Are you?"

"No. You must come for a visit. I'll teach you all about wine and winemaking."

"I'd like that." Camille's heart pounded at the thought of being with her again. "Do you see my cousin often?" Camille asked, amazed at how calm her voice sounded.

"It's hard for me to get away from my work. I'm only here in the city now because of business, but Marguerite and I do keep in touch."

"And how often do you get away?"

Nicole raised her head and looked at Camille curiously. "Seldom. Maybe once every three months."

"May I take you to the train station when you're ready to leave?"

"That's very kind of you, but won't Marguerite miss you?"

"Not at all." Camille seemed to be struggling for something else to say. She suddenly realized that she

24

was staring at her but couldn't stop. She had no desire to stop. "You have the bluest eyes," Camille heard herself saying.

Nicole smiled shyly and leaned against the railing beside her.

Chapter Four

The following day as Camille dressed for work she held a picture in her mind of Nicole stepping on the train. As the time had drawn nearer for her to leave, they had both grown more silent. Camille couldn't believe that she had let Nicole leave without getting at least a telephone number.

"She's gone," she mumbled, putting on her shoes and snapping herself back to the present, "and if you don't hurry, you'll be late again."

At work things were no better. Her concentration was sporadic and kept wandering back to Nicole. At ten o'clock Camille could stand it no longer; she called her cousin.

"Did I wake you?"

"Don't be silly," Marguerite said coolly. "When did the two of you slip out last night?"

"Oh, that." Camille drummed her fingers on a stack of folders on her desk. "We needed some air. When it was time for Nicole to meet her train, you were nowhere to be found." She trudged on bravely, sensing her cousin was in no mood for excuses or small talk. "I was wondering, Marguerite, if you had an address or a telephone number for your friend Nicole." Camille heard a clucking sound coming from the other end of the telephone.

"Strange you should ask. I received a call from Nicole not an hour ago. She wanted to apologize for leaving the party so abruptly without so much as a good-bye." Marguerite sounded more than simply irritated. "During the course of our conversation she just happened to ask for your telephone number."

Camille's heart skipped a beat. "We had a nice talk last night," she said calmly, even though her breathing had quickened.

"Nicole is a warm and wonderful person," Marguerite said. Camille could hear the rustling of pages in the background and moments later Marguerite gave her Nicole's address and telephone number. "She has a perfectly charming renovated château with a winery right next to it. You simply *must* see it, dear."

"She's invited me," Camille said casually.

"Nicole's very dedicated to the family business," Marguerite said. "Even more so since her father became ill. She works too hard and seldom gets away. Go if you can, Camille. She's very dear to me."

Camille busied herself at work, but the day passed slowly. That evening she took her work home, settled down a bit, and had a light supper. She finally fell asleep in her chair and didn't wake up until late. No one had called.

Several days passed and Camille continued working on her courage to call Nicole first. During the day she kept busy at the office, while in the evenings she read manuscripts and waited for the telephone to ring. Finally on Wednesday evening she got around to going through her mail and found an envelope with unfamiliar handwriting on it. She held the letter carefully by its edges and inspected it thoroughly. Inside was an invitation from Nicole to come to the château for a personal tour of the winery. The note stated that someone could meet her at the train station or that anyone in the village would be able to give her directions should she choose to drive. The note also stated that accommodations at the château were quite comfortable should she wish to stay a few days. It was short, to the point, and had been posted on Monday.

Camille felt ecstatic just touching the envelope. Its sweet smell gave her the courage to pick up the telephone and call her. They made arrangements for Camille to drive out on Friday evening.

The remainder of the week passed by slowly. Camille had to force herself not to call again just to hear that wonderful voice. On Friday afternoon she had everything in her car and was ready to go. The long hours she had spent working during the previous evenings had paid off considerably and allowed her some free time now for herself.

The village was over an hour's drive from Paris, with scenery and greenery that Camille had never taken the time to enjoy. Upon reaching the village, she stopped at a café to ask for directions. Camille sketched a small map on a piece of paper, careful to write down everything the café owner said. Darkness had set in, and she was worried about getting lost.

It was eight-thirty before she found her way to the château and knocked on the huge wooden door. She was greeted by a young woman and led through a hallway into a beautiful library.

"Mademoiselle Cartier has arrived," the maid announced.

Camille stepped into the library and found Nicole behind her desk. A fire was burning brightly in the enormous marble fireplace beside her. Camille eyed with slight envy the dark walnut bookcases lining every wall, filled with richly bound books. Several Persian rugs scattered about the room added splashes of brilliant color to the otherwise serious decor.

"Thank you, Claudette," Nicole said to the maid.

She stood up, smiled warmly, and went to the door to ensure that it was closed properly. "How was your trip?"

"Relaxing," Camille said. "I like the country. Burgundy is beautiful this time of year."

"Burgundy is always beautiful. Make yourself comfortable. I'm pleased that you could come."

"Marguerite has told me many wonderful things about this place. It's charming," Camille said sincerely as she settled into the deep-red velvet sofa and took in the exquisite antique furnishings. She had an almost irresistible urge to kick off her shoes and sink her toes into the thick carpet.

"Would you like some wine? Tea perhaps? Have you eaten?"

"Wine would be nice," Camille said, and leaned back and smiled. "Jeton wine?" she asked as she took the glass Nicole handed her.

"A good vintage, too." Nicole sat on the sofa also.

"You aren't having any?" Camille sipped the wine and found it no different from any other she had tasted. This disappointed her a little.

"A winemaster rarely drinks for pleasure." Nicole smiled. "But I might join you for a glass later."

"What does a winemaster do for pleasure?" Camille asked as those wonderful blue eyes scanned her once again with interest.

"I enjoy riding," Nicole said after a moment. "The stables are where I love to spend most of my time. Do you ride?"

"Yes," Camille said. "It's been years, though."

"We could go tomorrow if you like."

Camille expressed an interest in seeing more of the château, and Nicole was delighted to show her.

They left the library and ambled down the corridor, Nicole explaining the château's history and various techniques used in its latest renovation. As they walked back toward the foyer, the front door opened and a man in his mid-thirties came in.

"Antoine," Nicole called, "this is Camille Cartier. The friend I told you about from Paris."

Antoine crossed the room in a few strides. Camille eyed him carefully. He was tall and handsome, with dark wavy hair that slightly hung over his ears. She noted his serious brown eyes and a pleasant smile as he shook her hand.

"Our guest," he said. "I hope you enjoy your stay." He turned to Nicole and said, "Everything is secure. I'll see you both tomorrow. Nice meeting you. Good night." He took the stairs two at a time and was gone.

Camille was surprised to see him, having believed that Nicole lived alone. She couldn't remember, however, where she had gotten that idea. Nicole had said she was not married and hadn't mentioned living with anyone. A deep sense of disappointment washed over her as she tried to recall their conversation on the veranda the other evening. Camille was ready to admit the possibility that she had indeed made a mistake in her assumption.

"More wine?" Nicole asked as she opened the huge door to yet another room. They went inside and Camille was astonished at its uniqueness. All the furniture was done in royal blue, and a fire was already burning in the intricately carved black-marble fireplace. "I'll join you this time." Nicole brought their glasses back to the sofa.

"This is just fabulous," Camille said as she stared

about the beautiful room. "Marguerite told me what to expect, but she hardly did it justice."

"Thank you," Nicole said quietly. Camille noticed how she again ran the glass of wine under her nose several times before taking a sip.

Camille continued to absorb the elegance of the room, slowly studying the furniture and blue velvet drapes. Her gaze lingered on a portrait that hung over the fireplace. It bore a strong resemblance to Nicole, but the subject of the painting was ten to fifteen years older. Camille guessed it to be Nicole's mother possibly.

"The portrait looks remarkably like you."

Nicole looked up at the painting and smiled fondly. "I had it restored last year. That's Eva Jeton, my grandfather's sister. She met with a tragic death." Nicole stared at the fire, again sniffing the wine in her glass. "She was murdered by her brother. I've always felt very close to her."

Camille tried not to show her alarm at Nicole's casualness at such an unfortunate ending. "She's beautiful," Camille said. "The resemblance is uncanny."

Nicole seemed not to notice the indirect compliment. Gazing at the portrait, Nicole continued. "The circumstances of her death nearly tore the family apart. She was truly a fascinating woman."

"All families need someone fascinating," Camille said. "My family has Marguerite." She laughed and then added, "I have an uncle who went to jail for driving a police car into a fountain. And he wasn't a policeman. When the family gets together we make him sit in a room by himself. No one claims to know who he is." The sound of Nicole's laughter was like music in the air.

"You have an unusual way of expressing yourself." Nicole looked at her openly without showing any trace of embarrassment.

Camille concentrated on her wine, no longer able to meet those blue eyes that left her feeling so flustered and uncertain. She was still bothered by the thought of Antoine possibly waiting for Nicole upstairs. *How did I get myself into this?* she wondered. There were so many questions she wanted to ask, and so many things she wanted to say.

"Why do you do that?" Camille asked suddenly, seeing Nicole sniff the wine again. "Am I not supposed to drink this?"

Nicole smiled and explained, "It's just a habit. The smell of wine prepares the palate for what is to come. The smell is usually better than the taste. Try it."

Camille sniffed what was left in her glass and then sipped the wine. "Tastes the same to me."

"You have an untrained nose," Nicole said. "You'll grow accustomed to it. I'll teach you."

"Tell me about winemaking." *That should keep the lovely voice going for a while,* Camille thought, and she was right. They talked on into the wee hours of the morning, mostly about wine. Nicole finally insisted that Camille explain her job at the magazine.

"The life of a junior editor is relatively boring." Her head was beginning to buzz from the wine, and she noted that Nicole was still working on her first glass.

"You must be tired," Nicole said suddenly. "I have a long day planned for us tomorrow. Let me show you where your room is." Camille followed her up the stairs slowly while Nicole answered questions about the château and various furniture pieces.

The second-floor hallway was covered in thick, rust-colored carpet. Three elaborate chandeliers bathed the hallway in sensuous light, making it difficult for Camille to keep her gaze from drifting to Nicole's long, supple body. They passed two doors before Nicole stopped.

"This room is yours," she said. "My room is the one on the end." She opened the door and went in, switching on a lamp. "Sleep as late as you like. Claudette will know where to find me in the morning." Nicole moved across the room and flipped on the light to the small bathroom on the left. Camille suddenly felt uneasy with their unintentional closeness. With determination, she forced herself to concentrate on her suitcase at the end of the huge four-poster bed.

"This is lovely," Camille said. "Thank you."

Their eyes met briefly. Nicole looked away first and said, "I'm at the end of the hall if you need me. I'll see you in the morning."

Camille dressed for bed, too excited to sleep. She settled comfortably in the dark thinking of nothing but Nicole: those wonderful blue eyes and that hair with its unusual mahogany patches that cascaded past her shoulders. "And she lives with a man," she said as she tried to get comfortable.

Camille eventually drifted off to sleep as the moonlight filtered in through the window. The temperature in the room dropped sharply, causing her to burrow deeper into the warmth of the covers. Suddenly she sensed that she was not alone, and that someone was near the bed.

Camille tried to wake up, but was caught in the heavy cloud of sleep. With great effort she pulled her eyes open and caught a glimpse of blue slowly moving near the door. It looked like a woman, but the apparition faded in and out rapidly before quietly vanishing altogether. Camille stopped fighting and drifted back to sleep, convinced it was all a dream brought on by her overindulgence of wine. Whoever or whatever it had been was not there to harm her. She tugged on the blanket and again was fast asleep.

Chapter Five

Camille slept peacefully until a ray of sunshine crept through a small gap in the drapes. She looked at her watch on the table beside the bed and was surprised to see it was a little after nine. She showered quickly, dressed, and hurried downstairs, meeting Claudette coming out of the kitchen area.

"Breakfast, Mademoiselle?"

"Coffee, please. Emergency coffee, in fact." Camille followed her into the smaller of the two dining rooms.

Claudette pulled out a chair for her and returned

shortly with a service of coffee. "Mademoiselle Jeton will be here soon," she said as she poured. Camille was left alone with her coffee and noticed there was another cup on the tray. A few minutes later Antoine came in wearing shined shoes and brown coveralls.

"Good morning," he said brightly. "Nicole sent me over to get you. She's stuck on the telephone with a buyer and couldn't get away." He seated himself across from her and poured coffee into the other cup. Camille smiled, trying not to show her disappointment at having to share breakfast with him instead of Nicole. Claudette returned with an assortment of sliced fruit and cheeses.

"Mademoiselle Jeton would like to have the picnic lunch ready by eleven-thirty," he said. Claudette nodded and left. "How did you sleep?" he asked Camille.

"Very well, thank you. I can't believe how late it is already. I'm usually up much earlier."

"Nicole is very eager to show you the winery. I usually conduct the tours, but she insists on doing yours." He smiled. Camille again felt a nagging disappointment at his being there in Nicole's place. His confidence was only making things worse.

"You're from the city," he said stirring his coffee. "I lived in Paris for years and loved it."

"I like it, too."

"I understand you work for a magazine."

She was surprised and once again not altogether pleased that he and Nicole had already spent enough time together this morning to discuss her and her career. "I'm a junior editor. Very boring."

"Nonsense," he said with a laugh. "What could be more boring than waiting for grapes to grow?"

Camille found herself liking him despite his possible involvement with Nicole. They finished their coffee, and Antoine escorted her to the winery.

Camille was immediately impressed by its cleanliness and organization. She spotted Nicole in the corner wearing a white lab coat, a light blue turtleneck sweater, and a pair of dark blue slacks. She was going over charts with three men who were listening as she explained something to them. Seeing Camille she waved and finished with the group quickly.

"Thank you, Antoine," Nicole said as he took the charts from her. "Did you sleep well?" she asked Camille.

"Yes, very well." Camille glanced around curiously. "So this is where it all begins?"

"This is it," Nicole answered. "I'll show you how everything works. We'll start at the beginning, so you'll have some idea of what I'm talking about." Camille followed her down a hallway near the back of the winery. "Pretend we've just harvested the grapes," Nicole said. She went on to explain where and how the grapes were delivered before they were washed and how the clean grapes were pressed and the juice saved. An hour later they had already covered the nursery where sprigs were tended and had toured the room where the vats were kept.

"The vat room?" Camille said. "It sounds like a caped crusader should live there."

A while later they were underground in the cellar where the casks were stacked and stored. The lighting was dim in the cellar and the temperature there very cool. Camille was reminded of her dream the night before, the splash of blue near the door, and the coolness that had so suddenly come over her.

"Once the wine is ready," Nicole said, "we sell it and ship it out in these." She rubbed a wooden cask fondly. "It's bottled, corked, and labeled somewhere else. The Jeton name never appears on the label." Nicole smiled. "Those interested in the Jeton Vineyards keep track of whom we sell to."

Camille was fascinated with the bottling practices. "I've never heard of such a thing. The label has nothing to do with where the wine comes from?"

"Usually not."

"It sounds almost deceitful!"

Nicole laughed. "We get good prices. The wine industry knows the quality of our product. Buyers come to us." Nicole put her hand on Camille's shoulder as she led her through the rows of stacked barrels. Camille was very conscious of their closeness as they stopped at the base of the stairs leading up to the other floors.

"How do you know when the wine is ready to sell?" Camille asked.

Nicole removed her hand. "We taste it periodically," she said. The dim light was reflected in her pale blue eyes, and Camille felt herself being drawn even closer. "A winemaster knows when the time is right," Nicole said quietly.

Camille felt pure desire at that moment and knew instinctively that Nicole was feeling the same thing. *It would be so easy to kiss her,* Camille thought. *So easy.* But not knowing exactly where Antoine fit into this woman's life made Camille more cautious than usual. She wasn't ready to risk making a fool of herself yet.

Camille had allowed too much time to pass, and the moment was gone. Nicole looked away from her. "I'll show you the lab next," she said as she slowly started up the stairs. "Now that you know all about winemaking," she teased, "it's time to educate you on how to drink it. Few people realize how much better it tastes when certain steps are followed."

On the first floor Camille saw Antoine with a tour of about thirty people, several with cameras around their necks and brochures in their hands. His deep voice carried well. Camille realized how fortunate she was to have had a much more personal tour. They climbed another flight of stairs to the next floor where several offices and a large laboratory were located.

"In here," Nicole said as she opened a door and turned on the light, "is where we do soil samples and pH testing. The fermentation process has to be monitored frequently."

Camille saw several test tubes with an inch or so of dirt and others with wine samples of various colors. Nicole closed the door; they proceeded on across the hall to another office. Camille was still surprised at how clean and orderly everything was. From the outside the winery looked like no more than a large old barn, but inside it was new, spotless, and very well organized.

"How many employees do you have?"

"There are ten of us including myself and Antoine. We all work together very well." Nicole switched the light on in her office and closed the door. "We're more like a family than a business."

Camille saw two wine glasses about one-third full of red wine setting on the desk. The office was small and contained several bookcases filled with volumes of labeled notebooks.

"As in any other business, winemaking has mountains of paperwork," Nicole said, seeing Camille looking at the notebooks. "Each harvest has its own history recorded. Daily temperatures and rainfall are logged. Even after the wine is sold, we keep the records of how it progressed." Nicole went to the desk and picked up the two wine glasses. "Ready for your first lesson?"

Camille smiled and took the glass from her, conscious of their fingertips touching briefly. Nicole leaned against her desk and gingerly held the glass.

"Never gulp," Nicole said with a smile. "Swirl and smell." The wine in her glass began to slosh a little as she moved her hand slightly. Camille followed her instructions. "Smell the wine slowly," Nicole instructed. "Swirl it and smell a few times before taking any in your mouth. Once it's in your mouth, leave it there a few seconds so your palate is satisfied. Try it. See how it tastes."

The sheer sensuality of the entire process was delightful. Camille swirled and sniffed the wine, and took a generous sip into her mouth. She swished it around and was pleasantly surprised at how receptive her taste buds had been. It was by far the best mouthful of wine she had ever tasted.

Camille nodded. "It was well worth the trouble."

They finished their wine and left for the stables

where two horses were saddled and ready when they arrived. Claudette was there with a lunch packed for them.

"We'll be by the river and back by dark," Nicole told the maid as she climbed into the saddle. "Have Antoine take any calls that can't wait." Turning to Camille she said, "We'll ride by the vineyard on our way to the river." The horses trotted off side by side.

Camille didn't realize how much she had missed riding. As they drew closer to the vineyard, she became lost in the beauty of the landscape as acres and acres of vines in their uniform rows came into view.

"This is marvelous!"

"It's one of my favorite places," Nicole said. "When my brother and I were younger we'd ride up here and sit for hours. The river isn't far," she said, urging the horse into a trot. Camille followed and enjoyed the sight in front of her: the vineyard, the horse, and the woman who was quickly stealing her heart.

They had ridden about fifteen minutes before hearing the river. Trees lined and shaded the bank where they walked their horses. Nicole spread a blanket and busied herself with the lunch, while Camille found a corkscrew and opened the bottle of wine. Two carefully wrapped glasses were unpacked and filled. Camille was careful to swirl and smell before tasting the wine; she flushed under Nicole's approving eyes.

Camille tossed back her shoulder-length hair and nibbled a piece of cheese. "Who exactly is Antoine?" she asked after a moment. The question had been nagging at her since last night, and she refused to wonder about the answer any longer.

Nicole stretched seductively on the blanket and swirled the wine in her glass. "Antoine is a friend of my brother's. They lived together for several years before my brother went away."

Lived together, Camille mused. *That could mean any of several things, or it could mean absolutely nothing at all.* She sensed Nicole watching her closely, as if waiting for something, but Camille had already been as bold as she felt comfortable being.

"Antoine is a very good friend," Nicole said.

"Where is your brother?"

"We never know. He shows up about every two years or so. It's been about that long since we saw him last. We expect him at almost any time now." Nicole finished her wine and poured more into their glasses. "He worked at the winery after my father became ill, but Lalo tired of it quickly. Why are you so curious about Antoine? You seemed surprised to see him last night when he came in."

"Marguerite told me you lived alone," Camille said matter-of-factly.

"Marguerite knows very little about me, actually." Once again their eyes met. "Lalo and Antoine were lovers," Nicole said easily. Her voice was soft and flowing, adding more meaning to her words. "Does that shock you?"

"Few things shock me," Camille said honestly. She breathed a sigh of relief and realized that Antoine was suddenly a much more likable person. Camille continued swirling her wine, stalling while she collected her thoughts.

"Nothing shocks you?" Nicole asked as she set her glass down and moved the cheese and pastries out of the way. "I brought you here to seduce you. Does that shock you?"

Camille felt a thousand butterflies burst to life in the pit of her stomach as Nicole's words began to sink in. "Nothing shocks me," she answered hoarsely. The wine in her glass stopped swirling; she set it down carefully. Camille lay back on the blanket, her body offering its own invitation. With slow deliberation Nicole moved towards her and straddled Camille's waist. She leaned over to kiss her, and their lips met hesitantly at first, and then hungrily. Nicole's inquisitive tongue readily convinced Camille that this was more serious than she could ever have imagined. The wine glasses tipped over onto the thick lush grass, but neither of them noticed.

With Camille on her back holding Nicole's soft, determined face in her hands, their kisses continued on in a deep, complete merging of passion.

"My dear, beautiful friend," Nicole murmured as her fingers began to slowly unbutton Camille's blouse.

Camille surrendered to a burning desire. The sheer pleasure of having those talented hands on her skin, and the dexterity with which Nicole freed them both of their clothing heightened their enjoyment.

Camille's blouse was tossed somewhere behind them, and various other articles of clothing followed soon after. She knew the look in Nicole's eyes as she gazed down at her. There was that playful smile and a sense of wonder in her expression. Camille tugged on Nicole's sweater and pulled it over her head. They both helped with the scramble to remove the rest of each other's clothing. With anticipation and longing,

Nicole leaned over once more and let their bare breasts touch.

"You're beautiful," Nicole whispered. She reached for Camille's hair and then trailed a delicate finger down across her cheek. Nicole brought her mouth down to an ample breast, letting the tip of her tongue circle the firm, swollen nipple.

"Wine isn't the only thing you've mastered," Camille said as she pulled Nicole even closer. She drank in the sweet scent of her thick, auburn hair and felt totally consumed in the passion between them.

It was dusk before they returned to the stables.

Chapter Six

After a hot bath and fresh clothes, Camille met Antoine and Nicole for dinner in the formal dining room. As she came in, Antoine stood and pulled her chair out for her. He had changed from his coveralls into tan slacks and a pale yellow open-collar shirt. Nicole remained at the head of the table with Camille and Antoine at the corners on either side of her.

"Did you enjoy your ride this afternoon?" he asked pleasantly.

"Yes, very much," Camille managed to say, knowing without a doubt that she was blushing. She purposely avoided looking in Nicole's direction.

"Nicole tells me you went to the river. It's lovely there."

"Yes, very." Camille finally glanced over at her and felt a wave of desire engulf her all over again as they smiled at one another.

Claudette came in bringing their feast, pouring wine, and refilling bowls. Camille was famished.

"Only three tours scheduled for tomorrow," he said to Nicole. "I'll check the crop in the morning."

"You work seven days a week?" Camille asked them both.

"Only during the tourist season," Nicole said, "and during the harvest."

Antoine groaned playfully. "The harvest is twenty-four hours a day, seven days a week!"

Claudette entered a while later with coffee for them. "Your call came through, Monsieur," she said.

Antoine folded his napkin and stood up. "Excuse me. I'll only be a moment."

Claudette collected empty plates and served them dessert before leaving.

As Nicole sipped her coffee, her eyes met Camille's. "Would you stay in my room with me tonight? I want you very much."

Camille was speechless for a moment. She closed her eyes and took a deep breath as the tumbling in her stomach carried on. *Is it possible to be falling in love already?* she wondered.

"That would be wonderful," she said quietly, "but right now we must talk of other things if I have to wait any length of time before being with you again."

Nicole laughed. "We can talk about anything you like."

Camille attempted to pull herself together. Grasping for something neutral to talk about, she asked how old the château was.

"It was built over three hundred years ago. It's been completely restored five times."

"It's charming," Camille said, still in awe as she took in the chandelier over the huge table.

"My great grandfather held the title of *Marquis* when he was very young. He moved his family here and was given a vast amount of land along with the château. It's been in my family ever since." Nicole lowered her voice a little as she said, "There are only three Jetons left. War has not been kind to us." She pushed her coffee aside and poured more wine into their glasses. "Is there anyone in your life at the moment?"

"No," Camille said quickly, glad that she could give that answer. "You promised we would talk about something else."

Claudette came in to see if they needed anything.

"Mademoiselle Cartier and I are retiring for the evening. We wish not to be disturbed for any reason," Nicole said without taking her eyes from Camille.

"Yes, Mademoiselle."

They left the dining room and started up the stairs. Camille could hear Antoine's muffled voice on the telephone in another room. Nicole took her hand and held it as their shoes sank into the thick carpet. Once inside Nicole's room they fell into each other's arms and kissed hungrily.

"This is all I've been able to think about,"

Camille whispered as she helped Nicole out of her sweater. Camille kissed her throat and grew weak at the delicate scent of her perfume.

"You've had many women," Nicole said. She took Camille's hand and led her across the room to the bed. "I'm very possessive."

Camille kissed her shoulder and slowly worked her way down to a breast, licking and sucking gently as Nicole's fingers toyed with her thick brown hair. It had been months since Camille had endured such bliss. She kissed the softness of Nicole's stomach and eventually reveled in the taste of her. She gently probed with her tongue, remembering having wanted to do this the first night they had met.

"Oh, yes . . . ," Nicole murmured as she clutched the corner of her pillow with one hand, while burying the other in Camille's hair. "Yes . . ." Her voice trailed off and her breathing quickened.

Camille heard the moans and felt the insistent, almost desperate thrashing movements of Nicole's body as she came. Camille was still for several minutes afterwards, savoring the feel of Nicole's warm, wet skin against hers.

"Come here," Nicole said in a small voice. "I need to hold you." She pulled Camille deeper into her arms and held her there for a moment. "We could have been here like this yesterday. Why did we wait?" She rolled Camille over on her back and settled comfortably on top of her. Camille tilted her head back, offering her throat easily, deliberately. It took hours before the urgency went away.

* * * * *

Camille stirred and felt arms tighten around her. She slowly opened her eyes to the light seeping into the room and Nicole's lips brushing the edge of her hair. "How long have you been awake?"

"Not long," Nicole whispered. She gently ran the tip of her finger down Camille's cheek. "Go back to sleep."

"Sleep?" Camille kissed her slowly and moved her hand down the length of Nicole's body. "I can sleep in Paris."

They made love quickly, passionately, with an intense, surprising thoroughness. As they settled into a more leisurely form of lovemaking, Camille had a new understanding of herself and what she wanted. The longer they were together, the harder it was going to be for her to leave.

There was a light knock on the door. Camille jumped and pulled the cover snugly up around her nude body.

"That's our breakfast," Nicole said. "Claudette's very punctual."

Camille watched her put on a robe and answer the door. Nicole returned with a tray and came back to the bed.

"Are your servants accustomed to you having strange women in your room?" Camille asked.

"Not at all," Nicole said with a laugh. "You're the first actually."

The tiny seedlings of jealousy were already making themselves known. "The first for this room?"

Nicole's hearty laughter made her feel a little better. "For any room. How often do you think I do this sort of thing?"

Camille shrugged. "Four or five times a week."

Nicole chased her around the bed with a cream puff. They fed each other morsels of cheese, bites of sweet rolls, and slices of fruit. It wasn't long before Camille had Nicole's robe off again and tossed on the floor.

"What must your servants be thinking?" Camille murmured as she nuzzled into the soft crook of Nicole's neck. "I'm never very quiet when I make love."

"My servants," Nicole said with some difficulty as a result of all the attention, "are probably in total agreement about how lucky I am at this very moment."

"You think so?"

"I'm positive. Claudette and the cook are lovers. They share quarters in another part of the château and they know exactly what we're doing no matter how much noise you make. Now come here and let me do that to you this time."

A while later Camille settled once again into her arms. "I need to be getting back," she said reluctantly.

"So soon?" Nicole glanced at the clock on the other side of the room. "Where has the time gone?"

Camille kissed her playfully on the tip of the nose. "We've used it wisely."

They took what was supposed to have been a quick shower together, but twenty minutes later they were still necking shamelessly under the spray.

As they dressed, Camille tried not to think about the upcoming week and being away from her. Even though their time together had been delightful, she was still unwilling to assume that an open invitation to return would be extended.

51

Camille spied a picture of a handsome young man on Nicole's dresser. The same twinge of jealousy that Antoine had aroused in her a few days before had returned. "Who is this?" she asked as she picked up the picture.

"Lalo. My brother," Nicole said.

"He's a nice looking man."

Nicole took her by the hand and led her to the door. "I have something interesting to show you," she said, "but first there's someone I'd like for you to meet before you go."

They entered the room next to the one Camille had stayed in her first night there. It smelled wonderfully of roses. Camille saw the beautiful flowers on a small table in the corner. The nurse sitting near the window smiled and got up to leave.

"Papa," Nicole said quietly, "I've brought a friend to see you."

The frail, withered man opened his eyes but did not speak. Nicole sat on the edge of his bed and took Camille's hand and pulled her closer. Camille listened as Nicole told him of tourists visiting the winery, their ride to the river and dinner with Antoine. There was no acknowledgment in his eyes that he understood anything she was saying, but Nicole's tone of voice and the importance she gave to seemingly trivial things touched Camille deeply.

Nicole brushed his steel gray hair away from his forehead with her fingertips. "Rest now, Papa. I'll be back to sit with you later."

In the hallway Nicole took Camille's hand again and held it tightly for a moment. She seemed to be composing herself. "He's had two strokes. I'm the only one who thinks he can hear me."

Camille squeezed her hand. "He probably can."

Nicole led her down the hall past the staircase to a huge door that revealed another wing of the château. "We never use this section any longer unless we're expecting several guests." Nicole found a light switch that lit up a long hallway identical to the one they had just stepped out of. The carpet was the same rust color, and chandeliers ran the center of the high ceiling.

"Just how big *is* this place?" Camille asked in amazement. The hallway seemed to go on forever.

Nicole took her hand once more and held it reassuringly. "There are rooms here in the château that I haven't been in since I was a child. I don't have the time to really enjoy my home anymore."

They moved down the hallway together, Camille eyeing the marvelous antique furnishings that lined the walls. They stopped in front of a large portrait hanging across from several closed doors. It appeared to be a portrait of Lalo, Nicole's brother. The subject had light brown hair and brown eyes, but even though the hairstyle was much different from the photograph Camille had seen earlier, the features and determination were the same.

"This," Nicole said as she studied the painting closely, "is Philippe Jeton, my grandfather." Camille's hand gripped hers tightly as they stood gazing at the portrait. "He was Eva Jeton's brother. He strangled her one night. She died in this room behind us."

"Eva Jeton," Camille whispered. Where had she heard that name before?

"The portrait in the drawing room," Nicole said, as if reading her mind.

"The portrait that looks so much like you?"

Camille managed to say. She felt chills race up and down her arms. "This is a painting of your grandfather," Camille said slowly as she nodded toward the portrait on the wall, "and the one downstairs is a portrait of his sister?"

Nicole chuckled at her amazement but continued holding her hand.

"This is fascinating," Camille murmured.

They strolled back down the hallway with Camille occasionally glancing over her shoulder to get one last look at the painting. They stopped at the door, and Nicole leaned over to kiss her. Seconds later the temperature seemed to drop almost fifteen degrees as they embraced.

"Goodness," Camille whispered, and sank further into Nicole's arms seeking her warmth. "Why is it so cold in here?"

Nicole smiled and continued to hold her. "I wish you didn't have to go."

"I need to be at work early in the morning." Camille kissed her again, knowing how much she would miss not being able to see her for a while. "Your family sounds fascinating. I want to know all there is to know about you."

Nicole laughed. "You say that now," she teased. "Have you forgotten that my grandfather was a murderer?"

"None of us can choose her family," Camille reasoned. "That's why mine had to keep Marguerite."

They left the wing and collected Camille's luggage before going downstairs. "I have something you might find interesting," Nicole said. Camille followed her to the library where Nicole selected a thin book with a brown leather cover.

"This is Eva Jeton's diary. It's very interesting reading. It may tell you much more about us than you care to know."

Camille caressed it fondly and smiled at her, wanting to remember exactly what Nicole looked like at that very moment. *She's beautiful,* Camille mused. *I could drown in those blue eyes.* "I'll start it the moment I get back." Anything that would help her get to know this marvelous woman better certainly deserved her full attention, she decided.

"I wish you could stay longer," Nicole said. They walked to Camille's car arm in arm.

"This way we can get some sleep."

"Sleep is the farthest thing from my mind right now." Nicole opened the car door for her. "Call me when you get home."

Chapter Seven

Camille began reading the diary that evening after she returned to Paris. She became so absorbed in the life of Eva Jeton that she couldn't put it down until finishing the very last word. Eva's final entry had been recorded the night she died. Camille was so enthralled with the story that she reread the entire thing again at work the next day.

It was fascinating. Camille felt as though she had gotten to know Philippe Jeton, the murdering older brother, through Eva's words. Camille kept visualizing his portrait as she read. His thin, young face and slightly wild hair. There was something ruthless in his eyes, something dangerous, yet it was almost overlooked because of the boyishness of his handsome face. It was a disturbing tale.

Camille set the book down, her mind racing. The story saddened her as she thumbed through the pages once more. Her eyes fell on key phrases, phrases that reminded her of things Nicole had said during their brief time together. There was a bond between Eva and Nicole. As little as Camille knew about either of them, she was certain of that.

Camille reached for the telephone and called her cousin. Marguerite had apparently known the Jeton family at one time.

"Marguerite," she said, hoping to sound calmer than she felt.

"Camille, dear? You sound so strange. How was your trip to Burgundy?"

"Wonderful, thank you. I need some information." Camille began by asking her cousin if she knew anything about Nicole's brother.

"I only met Lalo once," Marguerite said. "I remember his being a very charming man. I never really bothered to ask where he ended up. I understand he no longer lives there at the château. He was an alcoholic. Can you imagine, Camille, dear? A winemaster with a drinking problem? The winery began losing money while he was in charge. Nicole has made it a success once again."

"What do you know of Nicole's parents?"

"Her mother died when Nicole was quite young, and her father became seriously ill while she was away at college. Lalo and Nicole had to take over the winery. It was said that Nicole had a better feel for the wine business than her brother did. Winemasters are usually old men, Camille. Believe me when I tell you that she is a gifted young woman."

"Yes, I know," Camille said thoughtfully. *How well I know.*

"Lalo has drunk and gambled away a fortune already. From what I understand, he returns to the château periodically to line his pockets. Nicole doesn't like to talk about herself or her family much. Whatever I know, I've had to pry out of her."

"The château is fabulous," Camille said.

"Oh, yes. It's beautiful. I haven't been there in a while, but I remember." Marguerite babbled on a few more minutes before they hung up.

Later that evening, thoughts of both Eva and Nicole Jeton seemed to merge together in Camille's mind. She remembered the portrait of Eva that she had seen over the fireplace that first night of her arrival. The portrait that looked so remarkably like Nicole. *How very unusual,* Camille thought. The next time she was there, if there indeed *was* a next time, she wanted to study Eva's portrait more closely.

Camille placed a call to the château, but the maid informed her that Nicole was working late. She promised to give her a message. Nicole finally returned the call a few hours later.

"I found myself swirling and sniffing a glass of water this morning," Camille said. Nicole's laughter was music at its loveliest. "How are you?"

"Lonely," Nicole said with a light laugh. "Did you read Eva's diary?"

"Three times already."

"How does it feel to know that you've made love to a woman descended from a murderer?"

"I haven't made love to her nearly so much as I intend to."

There was silence for a moment, then Nicole said, "When will I see you again?" Her voice was low and serious.

"When would you like to see me again?"

"Now if it were possible."

"Not possible."

"Then can you come Friday? Like before?"

"Yes," Camille said. She was finally able to relax a little now that it was evident that Nicole was interested in her also. "I'll call you tomorrow."

Nicole was having her morning coffee, preparing herself for a busy day inspecting the vineyards. Her crisp· riding outfit and shined boots would be covered with mud within the hour. She sipped her coffee and thought of Camille.

She wanted to be with her again and thought about it constantly, but as the days crept by it seemed more and more out of the question. The château was hardly the peaceful place it had been the week before. Eva was restless again. No one was getting much sleep. Intimacy would be hard to come by with a ghost in their midst. Keeping Camille away now was both necessary and at the same time one of the hardest things Nicole had ever had to do. She would have to call her this evening and cancel for the weekend.

Antoine came in, dressed in his coveralls, snatching up his napkin as he sat down. "Am I the only one she's keeping awake?" he snapped. "All night long she was in and out of my room! Isn't there something you can do about her, Nicole?"

"She's upset and anxious."

"Talk to her! *Some*thing," he barked.

Nicole ignored his ranting. She, too, had seen Eva several times during the night but had been able to sleep some anyway. Antoine was much more nervous about it, still unable to adjust completely to the strange happenings around the château.

"It's because of Lalo," he said as he poured his own coffee and splashed it all over the saucer. "She always does this before he comes back."

Nicole set her cup down. "We haven't heard from him. It might be something else." She pushed thoughts of her father and his weakening state out of her mind. Eva could be upset over a number of things.

Antoine looked at her sharply, his face stern only seconds before relaxing. "How much do you think Lalo will want this time?"

"I don't know. He took nearly everything last time."

"You look tired. Camille's visit will do you good."

"I'm going to call her and tell her not to come. I don't want her here while Eva's like this." Nicole reached over and touched his hand. "Eva has us all on edge. I'm sure this will pass very soon."

"I hope you're right. I'm exhausted."

Eva's antics increased, and neither Nicole nor Antoine got any sleep. The apparition continued to walk the upstairs halls at night, going from Nicole's room to Antoine's room and back. The temperature fluctuated so much that both were amazed they hadn't caught pneumonia. Eva's presence alone was annoying enough, something Nicole was not afraid of, but when the moaning began, Antoine decided he had had enough. He and Nicole met in the hallway, both dressed in their robes, neither having slept more than ten minutes in the last three hours.

"What is she *do*ing?" Antoine whined as he tied his sash. "She's never made noise before. That moaning! It's pathetic. Can't you *do* something with her? Talk to her?" There was an edge of fear in his voice. Nicole, obviously the emotionally stronger of the two, felt obligated to take control of the situation.

"Try to get some sleep in the library," she said. "I'll see what I can do up here."

Antoine returned to his room and got his blanket and pillow and gladly escaped downstairs. Nicole went back to her own room and sat on the edge of the bed, waiting for Eva to appear. With a sigh she bowed her head. How could she ever think of bringing Camille into something like this?

Camille worked vigorously through the week, rearranging her schedule and putting in extra hours. The work she failed to finish at the office went home with her. It helped to keep her mind free of Nicole and the brief time they had spent together. Those thoughts Camille saved for the few quiet moments she had just before drifting off to sleep in the wee hours of the morning.

Nicole called her Wednesday evening and informed her that something had come up. They wouldn't be able to spend the weekend together. Nicole had seemed quiet and distant. Camille's disappointment had prevented her from asking the questions that she felt compelled to ask. The next morning Antoine called to tell her that Nicole's father had died during the night.

"I suppose it's a blessing," he said.

"How is she?"

"Better. She's putting all her efforts into locating Lalo right now."

As Camille's mind raced with what she should do next, Antoine said, "Nicole has requested that there be no visitors outside of the family. This was her father's wish before he became so ill. Nicole asked me to tell you to please be patient. When things are more settled here, she will be in touch with you."

In touch? Camille thought. It sounded so impersonal.

"She needs this time, Camille. Things are bad here right now."

"I'll do whatever she wants, Antoine, but you must promise to call me if either of you needs anything."

"Yes, of course."

Every morning Claudette had flowers ready for Nicole as soon as she came downstairs. Nicole took them to the family cemetery behind the château and placed a few on her father's fresh grave and then some on her mother's. From there she was able to start the day.

Her tears still came occasionally, but her anger seemed to be with her constantly now. When Nicole had finally located her brother in Morocco to tell him their father was dead, Lalo had chosen then to elaborate on his upcoming plans to visit the United States. He had no intention of returning for the funeral and stated flatly that he had considered his father dead for many years already.

The château was quiet when Nicole returned from the cemetery. She went to the library to tend to the mail that had been piling up on her desk. She needed her work now more than she ever had in her entire life.

During the second week Camille was anxious about not having heard from Nicole or Antoine, but by the third week it was all she could do to keep herself away from the telephone. Finally she could stand it no longer and called the château one evening and was told by Claudette that Mademoiselle Jeton was working late. Camille left a message, but Nicole didn't return her call.

The next morning Camille telephoned the château from work, and the maid confided that Nicole seemed very distressed. She had been unable to eat, was working late hours, and was refusing to take any personal calls.

"She's near collapse," Claudette whispered in a secretive, concerned voice.

"Why doesn't Antoine help her?" Camille demanded.

"He stays gone when he's not working."

"Please tell Nicole that I called," she said quietly. Camille put the finishing touches on a plan of her own. She telephoned Marguerite for a much needed favor and spent the remainder of the evening packing and planning.

Early Friday afternoon Camille left Paris for Burgundy. The drive to the château was filled with uncertainty. She had no idea what to expect when she arrived, but she sensed that Nicole would not be happy to see her.

The rain sent tourists pouring from the bus and racing for the open door of the winery. Camille parked her car and hurried in among them. They were mostly young school girls shaking the rain from their hair like frisky puppies ridding themselves of bathwater. Camille stepped away from the chattering tourists and, feeling certain that Nicole would be there, briefly scanned the winery for her. Moments later she saw her looking stiff and formidable in her white lab coat, gray blouse, and black cotton slacks. Her auburn hair bounced on her shoulders as she passed a clipboard to one of the workers. Camille remembered the feel of that lovely hair in her fingers and its sweet clean smell as she held her. There was a tumbling in her stomach, but she wasn't sure if it was a result of seeing Nicole again or being nervous about showing up uninvited.

Camille watched Antoine come down the stairs and take Nicole by the arm. They seemed to be having words; Nicole was vigorously shaking her head. They stopped talking as they both saw Camille at the same time. Antoine smiled broadly and motioned for her to join them. Nicole only stared, her face carefully concealing any emotion.

Camille made her way through the noisy tourists and felt absolutely certain for the first time that day that her plan was the right one. Up close Nicole looked drawn and tired.

"What a pleasant surprise," Antoine said as he put his hand on Camille's back. "You must have gotten an early start."

"Yes, I did," Camille said over the buzz of the tourists. "I've come to take Nicole away for the weekend."

Antoine's hand moved to her shoulder and squeezed gently. "I think that's a wonderful idea."

"I'm not a child," Nicole said finally. "Stop talking about me as if I'm not here."

"Then you'll go?" he said, surprised. Camille had also expected to have a fight on her hands. In answer to his question, Nicole only threw her hands up in the air and grumbled in exasperation. She took her lab coat off and shoved it at him and marched abruptly out of the winery and into the rain.

Camille hurriedly gave Antoine a piece of paper. "This is where we can be reached if you need us. I'll have her back Sunday evening." Antoine took the note and stuck it in his pocket. He gave a little salute and smiled at her.

By the time Camille arrived at the château, Nicole was pacing in the foyer. They were both soaked and freezing. She stopped abruptly and crossed her arms.

"I said I would call you, Camille. What are you doing here?"

"Let's not argue about this," Camille said. "I've

made arrangements to take you away for a few days."

"I can't just leave! I have a business to run."

"Antoine's very capable. Don't you agree?"

Claudette came down the stairs with a suitcase and set it near the door.

"Thank you," Nicole said quietly. "Mademoiselle Cartier informs me that I'll be back in a few days." She snatched up the suitcase and stormed out the door and into the rain. Throwing her luggage in the backseat of Camille's car, she slammed the door.

Camille found this never-before-seen display of Jeton temper a little amusing but refrained from comment. In addition, she promised herself that she wouldn't mention anything about Nicole's father unless Nicole herself brought the subject up. *When she's ready to talk,* Camille reasoned, *she'll talk.*

The first fifteen minutes of their journey were spent in total silence. Camille drove steadily, and before long Nicole was asleep with her head resting back on the seat. Camille drove on through the rain, feeling relaxed as the rhythm of the wipers kept time with the soft music from the radio. Nicole woke up an hour later when they stopped for gas but didn't say anything until they were back on the road again. Camille could see that she was still terribly tired.

"Why are you so angry?" Camille finally asked her.

Nicole looked out the window at the rain. "Insurmountable reasons," she said in that soft, determined voice that Camille loved to hear. Then she added, "I hate rain."

As if Nicole's dislike for it were all the sky had been waiting for, it finally stopped raining. They reached Marguerite's villa a while later and set about exploring the premises and opening windows to air out the small estate. Marguerite promised they would have complete privacy.

"It's lovely here," Nicole said as they leaned over the small bridge and watched a few leaves being carried away in the stream.

"How long are you going to punish yourself for being here with me?" Camille asked.

Nicole dropped a pebble into the water and waited until the ripples subsided before answering. "Allowing time for myself has never been easy for me. It's especially hard now."

"Why now?"

"I don't know exactly."

"Just relax," Camille said as they began to stroll along the worn path back to the villa. Nicole reached for Camille's hand and then held it tightly, the first time they had touched all day. "You," Camille said slowly, "should be your one and only concern right now. Antoine can take care of things while you're gone. How about letting someone take care of you for a change? At least for a few days."

"It's so easy to be with you," Nicole said. "I'm sorry I've been difficult. Guilt is something I've never handled well."

"Why should you feel guilty about anything?"

Nicole smiled. She opened the door to the villa and continued holding Camille's hand. Camille saw an instant change come over her as they closed the door. "No one has ever offered to take care of me before. Even for a few days."

"I find that hard to believe," Camille said as Nicole pulled her into her arms. They held each other for a long time. Camille buried her face in the side of Nicole's neck where her lips kissed the softness of flesh. Within moments they had various articles of clothing in several stages of disarray. They broke away from each other long enough to find a bedroom close by and finished undressing quickly. Camille brought her mouth down to Nicole's breast and heard the subdued, cooing murmurs. Their bodies moved together in the velvety softness of a woman loving another woman. Words could wait. Camille knew all she needed to know for now.

Nicole, so easily brought to the brink of rapturous delight, soon gave way to Camille's desire to please her. Camille's lips and knowledgeable fingertips were everywhere, caressing and touching her with such insight and understanding that it seemed as though only moments passed before orgasm snatched her from reality and tossed her into oblivion. She called out Camille's name and reached for her. Nicole's breathing was labored but satisfied, and her drunken expression had such trust and tranquillity in it that Camille wanted nothing more than to stay in her arms forever.

After several minutes of necessary sleep for both of them, Camille woke up to Nicole's lips on her cheek.

"It's not always like this for me," Nicole whispered. She had such emotion in her voice that Camille wasn't sure if she would cry or not. "I feel so different with you. So different." She kissed Camille slowly, letting the softness of their lips arouse them both all over again. Camille squirmed delightedly under her, holding Nicole's face in her hands and loving those blue eyes that seemed to come to life so easily.

Nicole's mouth covered a nipple; she took her time and made love to her slowly. Camille gasped as Nicole's hand moved down her toned body, caressing her hip and the inside of her thigh. As Nicole's fingers touched the wetness, wonderful sounds of encouragement came from Camille's throat in a symphony of urgency and lust.

"Yes . . . there . . . ," Camille whispered huskily, her voice intense with desire. She held onto Nicole's small, bare shoulders and kissed them erratically, wanting more of her as the seconds ticked away. Her hands were in Nicole's long, thick hair, loving its softness and fresh orange blossom fragrance. Camille held her breath and ran her fingers along Nicole's back, pulling her even closer. Wave after wave of pleasure washed over her and lingered for the longest time.

Afterward, Nicole held her and they drifted to sleep, entwined in each other's arms. Camille snuggled and nuzzled into the soft curve of her neck and shoulder, feeling safe and wanted. They didn't stir for hours.

Chapter Eight

They spent most of the following morning in bed; neither was accustomed to this luxury. Camille fixed a late breakfast, and they laughed about the silliest things and touched often. Camille felt as though she had known this woman all her life. Being with her was so easy. It felt right in a way Camille had never experienced before. In what few other relationships she had been involved in, one of which had lasted three years, there hadn't been this closeness, this firm connection after only a few weeks. Camille was beginning to wonder if she had ever really been in love before.

They dressed and went for a walk in the woods, arm in arm down a path to a small, clear pond not far from the villa. They took off their shoes and waded in the cold water, playfully splashing each other. Camille showed little mercy when Nicole squealed for her to stop.

Their laughter merged with coughing and sputtering while water dripped from their soaked clothes. They waded back to the bank where Camille caught her in her arms and kissed her lightly on the lips.

"I remember a very pleasant interlude on a riverbank not long ago," Nicole said. Nimble fingers dealt with several buttons on Camille's blouse, and found a swollen nipple there waiting. Camille put her hands on Nicole's waist and pulled her closer. Nicole's tongue offered sensations that rekindled passion very quickly.

"Goodness," Camille murmured. She moved her hands along her lover's body to her thick, damp hair while Nicole continued unbuttoning the blouse and burying her face in Camille's breasts. Kisses became deep and lingering, their mouths receptive to whatever the other had to offer.

Soon they were lying down among nature's cushion of grass and leaves, neither of them caring about anything but the other. They were getting accustomed to each other's bodies, where giving pleasure became as urgent as receiving it.

Camille lowered herself onto Nicole's body and kissed her. Nicole accepted her tongue eagerly, avidly.

71

Camille's hands were everywhere, touching her with such love and perception that they both knew how wonderful it would be. Each time they made love was better than the last.

"You make me feel so different," Nicole said afterwards. "As if nothing else matters as long as I have you."

"Is that a bad thing?"

"Bad?" Nicole said. "No, not at all. Just different."

Camille raised herself up, arms outstretched on either side of Nicole's body. "I'm in love with you," Camille said.

Nicole was quiet, but she put her arms around Camille's neck and hugged her. Camille took the silence to mean that Nicole, in return, was not in love with her. She accepted that easily enough, rationalizing that it was much too soon. They had only known each other a few weeks.

They put themselves together again in silence and continued to walk in the woods until their clothes dried. Holding hands and stealing kisses kept them giggly and playful as they spotted rabbits and gathered firewood for the evening. Back at the villa, Nicole drew them a bath while Camille prepared a meal. They ate by candlelight, both clothed in robes and slippers, the leaves and twigs previously tangled in their hair now gone.

"I'm sorry we have no wine," Camille said. "I was certain I'd buy something thoroughly appalling."

Nicole's light laughter filled the room. Her hair was drying slowly with reddish locks falling across her forehead. "I'll be responsible for our wine in the future."

Camille smiled, taking notice of the term *our* wine in addition to a reference to the future. As darkness fell and they finished eating, Camille cleared away the dishes while Nicole started a fire in the fireplace. The day had passed quickly without so much as a word about the winery or Nicole's father. Nicole seemed to be temporarily set free from everything she had left behind. Camille imagined herself to be one of the few people ever to see this side of her and looked on fondly as she watched Nicole carefully build the fire.

Nicole's soft, delicate features were now in direct contrast to her usual image as a winemaster. *That lab coat reeks of authority,* Camille thought as she remembered Nicole standing on the stairs at the winery. *Authority is something she's learned to adjust to. It doesn't come to her naturally.*

When Camille returned she found the fire blazing and Nicole spreading an array of blankets and pillows in front of the hearth. Camille felt such joy and contentment. She moved up behind her, and they watched the fire in silence for a long time. Nicole turned and kissed her, and once again they made love.

"I can't seem to get enough of you," Nicole admitted. Their robes were open and their bodies bathed in the light from the fire. "Your eyes are the color of maple. They're so trusting. So knowing."

Camille reveled in the attention as Nicole leaned over her, kissing her throat easily while her hair brushed across Camille's breast.

"You've had many women," Nicole said.

Camille chuckled. "It's not true."

"How many?"

"Not many. I had a lover for three years."

"I hate her." There was laughter in Nicole's eyes as she gave her a hug. "I'm very possessive," Nicole said again. She moved her hand down Camille's stomach and over the soft mound that awaited attention so eagerly.

"I believe you," Camille whispered in short, raspy breaths. "You've pleased a few women yourself."

Nicole kissed her and gently rubbed her fingers into Camille's wetness. "You make me feel beautiful," Nicole whispered. "The way you look at me." She moved down slowly and replaced her fingers with her mouth. Camille's hands were in Nicole's soft, thick hair as she unconsciously showed her where she needed her the most.

As the moment came closer, Nicole acknowledged the hands in her hair, wanting her, guiding her to the point of no return.

"Wonderful," Camille whispered huskily. She spread her legs even farther apart and thrashed around like the wild nymph she imagined herself to be. The moment arrived and sent the explosion to every fiber of her being. Camille was too exhausted to do anything but tremble.

Nicole kissed her way up the paleness of Camille's stomach, lingering slowly over a breast before Camille took her in her arms. Tears were on her cheeks as she lay there in the warm glow of the fire.

"What are these?" Nicole asked softly. She rubbed her own cheek against the dampness.

"Happiness," Camille said. The reality of it's being their last night together was settling over her quickly. Camille dried her eyes on the back of her hand and sat up. She laid Nicole down among the pillows and enjoyed the sight of her in the flickering light of the fire. Nicole's blue eyes, seemingly so full of love, gave Camille the warmest, safest feeling she had ever known.

"You're a very passionate woman," Nicole said quietly.

"And you're a very good lover."

Nicole smiled and shook her head. "I've told you things I've never told anyone else. Something about you makes me trust you completely." She touched Camille's hair gently and smiled again. "I have so much to tell you. Things you probably care nothing about, but things I want to share with you anyway."

"By all means let's share," Camille said. She fluffed up the pillows and straightened the blankets a little, rearranging their nest to encourage conversation. Nicole pulled her into her arms and kissed her quickly several times on the top of the head.

"Are you comfortable?" Camille asked, settling easily against her.

"Very."

"Talk to me, Nicole. Tell me everything. Tell me about you and your family. Your dreams. Your ambitions."

"My ambitions?" Nicole said. "Thirty consecutive years of successful harvests would be nice. I have few if any ambitions. I'm doing what I love to do. How many people can say that?"

"Not many," Camille agreed. She herself certainly couldn't.

"It's not important that you believe everything that I tell you," Nicole said. "It's only important that I'm able to tell you. Can you understand that?" She ran a fingertip gently along Camille's arm and kissed her on the forehead. "Eva comes to me often," she whispered. "She's there in the château, walking the halls at night. She was there when I showed you my grandfather's portrait."

Camille trembled in her arms, and Nicole pulled a blanket up over them.

"She likes you. Don't be afraid." Nicole tightened her arms around her. "After my grandfather strangled her, he was never the same. It haunted him the rest of his life and he never quite recovered from it."

"Did you ever hear an explanation about why he killed her?"

"Several. The most commonly discussed has been jealousy," Nicole said. "Philippe was jealous of Eva's ability to run things without him. He would disappear for weeks at a time. No one knew where he was. There were rumors of a mistress and then rumors of foreign exports, but he never confirmed anything. Eva took care of the family business whenever he was gone. There was no one else able to do those things then. Their parents were old, and there were other children who were much younger." Nicole's voice was soft but steady. "One night Philippe returned after having been gone for a month. He rode up on his horse and stormed the stairs of the château to the second floor. He and Eva had a terrible quarrel. When the servants found them Philippe still had his hands clamped around her throat. She was dead."

Camille buried herself deeper into Nicole's arms. "What happened to him? Did he go to jail?"

"Nothing happened to him. The family kept it a

secret for years. With enough money you can buy silence." Nicole kissed the top of Camille's head again and rubbed her cheek against her hair. "Lalo, my brother, always wanted to be like him," Nicole continued softly. "He's wanted that more than anything. When he was younger Lalo would stare at the portrait for hours. He combed his hair the same way. Often wore similar clothes. He was so proud of the resemblance between them. He sees Philippe as this masculine hero who built the family fortune from nothing. My grandfather grieved for his sister for many years. They apparently had been very close when they were younger. Philippe finally married and became the man my father idolized and talked about. The Philippe Jeton the village remembers wasn't a murderer. He was a hero. And that's the man Lalo wants to be like. The hero." Nicole hugged her again and laughed. "But Eva's spirit never let any of us forget what really happened that night. Lalo has trouble accepting Eva's place in our family's history. I always remind him that there would be no Jeton Vineyards if Eva hadn't kept things going when Philippe would disappear for weeks at a time. My father eventually came to realize that I was right. Eva belongs there in the château as much as any of us do. Even now."

"I think I saw her once," Camille said. "My first night there."

"She was curious about you." Nicole tucked the blanket around them more snugly. She sighed and then continued. "Lalo and I were always so close when we were growing up, but we began drifting apart after Papa became ill. Something happened to my brother those first few months. He wasn't ready for the responsibility of running the winery. It scared him. Then he started drinking and would stay gone for several days and then weeks at a time."

"Like Philippe?"

Nicole hugged her again. "Yes. Like Philippe. Lalo spent all of his money, but always needed more. I loaned him some, but I got tired of that. I knew I would never see any of it again. After a while I made him sign for loans against what he would inherit if Papa died. Lalo would squander it all and make his way back home, happy to sign another note and be on his way again. He went through a tremendous amount of money, but there was no stopping him. The last time he was here I told him that was it. He had spent his share and then some. All the money that had been in trust for him was gone. And what did he have to show for it? Lalo's changed so much I hardly know him any more."

"How long has it been since you've seen him?"

"Three years," Nicole said.

"Does he know his father is dead?"

"He knows."

"You shouldn't have to go through this alone, Nicole. Your brother should be here with you."

Nicole kissed her cheek. "Here? Now?"

"Well, no," Camille said, momentarily flustered. "Not *here* here."

Nicole laughed. "My brother is a thirty-year-old child, Camille. Antoine has been more of a brother to me than Lalo will ever be." Nicole kissed Camille's ear and moved down her throat and bare shoulder. "No more talk tonight," she whispered huskily.

They spent the remainder of the evening making slow, thorough love to one another, and Camille knew in her heart that she could gladly spend the rest of her life doing the same.

The drive back to the château late Sunday afternoon was quiet and uneventful, but Camille could feel Nicole slipping away from her the closer they came to Burgundy. They held hands even though each was lost in her own thoughts. Nicole napped on Camille's shoulder briefly, their closeness a pleasant reminder of the time they had spent together.

Camille drove and thought of the Eva Jeton she had read about in the diary. She had never believed in ghosts before, but she reasoned that if Eva actually still roamed the halls of the château, she would probably be harmless. *Anything that looks so much like Nicole could never hurt anyone,* she mused. Yes, she believed Eva came back to visit. Part of the château's mystery and charm was probably due to Eva's presence there.

The car followed the winding road that led to the Jeton Vineyards, and Camille felt Nicole's hand tighten around hers. They parked in silence; Nicole carried her things inside.

Claudette was at the bottom of the staircase as they came in, and Camille noticed she appeared a bit frayed around the edges. Nicole set her suitcase down and paled when she saw her.

"The Marquis is back," Claudette said shakily. Her cheeks were flushed as she tugged on her starched apron.

Camille saw Nicole's expression turn to dread, but

Nicole didn't say anything. Camille reached for her, but Nicole eluded her grasp and marched toward the maid instead.

"Lalo is back?" she asked sharply.

"Yes, Mademoiselle," Claudette whispered in a small, terrified voice. "The hospital in Beaune. The Marquis took Antoine there."

"Lalo is *not* the Marquis!" Nicole said through clenched teeth. "The hospital?" she suddenly asked. "Did you say something about the hospital?"

"Antoine is there, Mademoiselle."

"What happened to Antoine? Is he all right?"

"There was an argument. Antoine hit his head."

Nicole went to Claudette and put her arm around her shoulder. "I'm here now," she said soothingly. "Everything will be fine." Nicole sat down with her at the foot of the stairs and gave her another reassuring hug. "Tell me exactly what happened. Take your time."

"The noises stopped as soon as you left, Mademoiselle." Nicole patted Claudette's hand, encouraging her to continue. "Yesterday morning the Marquis arrived with a young man. They came in and were very angry that you were away."

Camille watched the two women from a distance, admiring Nicole's calm reserve in action. The maid's fear and uneasiness had virtually disappeared with nothing more than Nicole's mere presence.

"Did my brother ask you to refer to him as the Marquis?" Nicole asked gently. When Claudette sniffed and nodded, Nicole hugged her again. "He is not the Marquis, and I don't want you calling him that. I'll speak to him about it. I promise you that Monsieur Jeton will not be a problem for any of

80

you." They stood up and Claudette dabbed at her eyes with the corner of her apron and adjusted her skirt.

Nicole started for the door with Camille right behind her. Outside they stopped and looked at one another.

"I'll drive you to Beaune," Camille said.

"No. You should be getting back to Paris. It's getting late."

"It's not that late. And besides, I'm worried about Antoine. Get in. I'll drive."

Chapter Nine

Nicole used the trip to prepare herself for what she would find at the hospital. She had wanted to protest and insist that Camille go home, but she didn't want to be alone. The reality of Lalo's being back had not quite settled in yet. She would have a better idea of how she felt about things once she saw him again.

She glanced over at Camille as she drove and was glad to have her there. *She says she's in love with me,* Nicole reminded herself. *But the timing is bad for us now. How can I ask her to become a part of this? Lalo could be so difficult when he wanted to be, and from the condition the servants had been found in, it was quite clear that he had not changed any.* Nicole looked out the window. She had no intention of exposing Camille to any of this.

At the hospital she asked what room Antoine was in and moved through the hallway quickly. She lowered her head as she maneuvered around cleverly placed carts and abandoned wheelchairs.

"I hate hospitals," she grumbled.

When they found Antoine's room, he was sitting up in bed with a small bandage on the side of his head. His eyes were red and his wavy hair a mess. Nicole went to him and kissed him on the cheek.

"What happened?" she asked gently.

"Lalo is back." He turned away from her. "He has a new lover."

Silence hung in the air between them. Nicole tried to think of something comforting to say to him, but words escaped her. She was forever surprised at how much Antoine still cared for her brother.

"I'm sorry," she finally whispered. "How are you? How did you get hurt? When can I take you home?"

"They'll release me tomorrow," he said solemnly. "Home, Nicole? I can't go back to the château with the two of them there." He socked his pillow a few times in an attempt to fluff it up before lying down and pulling the covers up under his chin. "Lalo's a sick man," he said as he closed his eyes. "You should have seen the way he pranced around, insisting on being referred to as the Marquis! He showed that young twit the winery. *His* winery, he kept saying.

His château. After all, he *is* the Mar*quis!*" Antoine, usually the more sedate and reasonable of the two, was nearly hysterical. "He's crazy, Nicole. Be careful."

"I can handle my brother," she said coolly. "And I won't stand for this nonsense about your not coming home tomorrow. Where is he, anyway? He wasn't at the château when I arrived."

"I saw him briefly earlier. I don't know where he is now."

"I'll be here in the morning to pick you up. Maybe I can talk to him tonight and see what he wants this time. Now tell me how you got hurt."

"We argued. I was upset." Antoine lowered his voice. "It was wonderful seeing him again, but at the same time I was terrified of him." He looked up and met Nicole's eyes. "You and I have discussed his coming back several times, Nicole, but each time it gets worse. This whole thing is only a game to him. One more way for him to be like his grandfather. He's sick, I tell you. He's *sick!*" Antoine squeezed her hand. "We had words when he introduced that imbecile he's calling his lover. The twit! Lalo didn't expect me to still be around, and he was angry that you were gone. We started shoving each other, and I hit my head on the stairs. I woke up here."

"I understand Eva was quiet once I left," Nicole said as she sat on the bed and gave his hand another comforting squeeze.

Antoine smiled for the first time. "Yes. We all slept well on Friday. The noises stopped."

"Lalo has obviously abused the servants during the short time he's been here. Do you remember any of that?"

"You know how he likes to yell at them. He was especially harsh with Claudette."

"I thought as much." Nicole got up from the edge of the bed. "I'll take care of my brother. You get well. I'll be here in the morning to take you home."

On the way back to the château Nicole was quiet as she formed a plan. She knew what had to be done concerning her brother and what would be best for Camille as well. Neither decision pleased her. She saw a strange car parked near the winery and felt a slight uneasiness in the pit of her stomach.

"It's very late," Nicole said. "Maybe you shouldn't go back to Paris until morning."

"Maybe I shouldn't go back at all," Camille said.

Nicole got out of the car and slammed the door. She leaned against it, not knowing what else to do. This was harder than she had thought it would be. Camille slowly got out of the car and went to her. They stood side by side in the darkness.

"I don't want you here," Nicole said softly. "Not now. Not like this."

"What am I supposed to do? I think you need me."

Nicole turned to her and saw the concern in Camille's eyes. *I shouldn't have let her take me to the hospital,* she thought. *That was a mistake.* "Go back to Paris. Wait for me to call you."

Camille was quiet as she stood there, her long, dark hair gently blowing in the breeze. "I can't do that," she whispered.

Nicole wanted to be held, wanted to feel this woman's hands on her again, but she couldn't let that happen. She had to clear her mind of such thoughts and concentrate on dealing with her brother. Lalo was something she needed to handle alone, without having to worry about anyone else right now. Nicole knew what she had to do, and she could think of no other way to convince Camille to leave.

"As I said before, it's late. You can stay the night." She started quickly for the château and shoved the heavy door open. Claudette was there at the bottom of the stairs, almost where they had left her earlier. She seemed startled by Nicole's swift determination. Camille came in behind her and closed the door.

"Please see that Mademoiselle Cartier is comfortable and has everything she needs," Nicole snapped. "She'll be leaving in the morning."

Camille was suddenly furious. "What are you doing?"

Nicole turned around and met Camille's fiery eyes. Nicole worked hard at making her stare icy and unfeeling. She had become an expert at it over the years.

"If you love me, you'll go back to Paris," Nicole said from the stairs, oblivious to the maid standing there trying to look as inconspicuous as possible. The lateness of the hour and the long drive back to the city were no longer factors during this discussion. They had moved on to something else already.

"And if you love me," Camille said slowly, "you'll let me stay and help you."

Nicole glared at her coldly and said, "Don't

confuse sex with love, Camille. Go back to Paris where you belong." She turned and hurried up the stairs, feeling a wrenching in her heart as she heard the thunder of the front door slamming. Somehow, through her own tears, she convinced herself that this was best. Lalo would take all of her energy. If she was to ever have any sort of a future again with anyone, she had to settle things with him first.

Nicole pulled herself together and tried to forget the devastated look on Camille's face. *She gives me the most wonderful weekend of my life and I treat her worse than anyone I've ever known,* Nicole thought as she patted her face dry and inspected her reflection in the mirror. On her dresser the picture of Lalo caught her eye. She picked it up and tossed it in a drawer.

She went downstairs, her hand sliding along the smooth banister as her shoes sank into the carpet. Claudette was in the foyer still wringing her hands in a jerky, nervous motion. Nicole gave her a warm smile and tried to put the young girl at ease. Nicole watched as Claudette visibly relaxed and let her hands fall to her sides.

"He's in the library, Mademoiselle," she said quickly. "Would you like something to eat? The cook can —"

"No. That will be all for this evening." Nicole touched the young girl's shoulder. "Everything will be fine. There's no need to worry."

Nicole felt confident as she went to the library. Before she got there she briefly examined her feelings about her brother. She suspected that her visit with Antoine had hardened her considerably. Lalo's games had always irritated her, but his refusal to return for their father's funeral was inexcusable. And the way he always turned the château into such chaos infuriated her; there was no excuse for it. He was complicating her life before she even had a chance to see him again. Nicole had to get things taken care of with him before she could begin to think about the mess she had made of her relationship with Camille. She felt a sinking in her heart at the words she had shouted at her. Hopefully the damage done had not been irreparable. The slamming door had been like a slap in the face and was still ringing in her ears.

Nicole went into the library and found Lalo behind her desk going over the ledgers. He looked the same, his sandy hair maybe a little longer and his face a tad thinner. *He looks good,* she decided as she watched him read the pages. He glanced up and then smiled.

"Nickie," he said as he stood up.

The sound of his voice and hearing him refer to her by that name brought sudden, unexpected tears. Lalo was the only person to ever call her Nickie, and it softened her immediately. She couldn't move for a moment as he came around her desk and reached for her. Nicole went to him and let herself go as his big arms went around her.

"Nickie," he said again, "aren't you glad to see me?"

She stiffened in his grasp and put her palms on his chest. His voice. His cologne. His smile. All the wonderful things she remembered about him meant nothing now as she looked up at him.

"How much do you want, and how long will you be staying?" She dabbed her eyes quickly as her anger began to return. Lalo moved away from her.

"Why is Antoine still here?" he asked. "I thought for sure he would have left by now."

"Your first questions are about Antoine? Not Papa? He's dead, Lalo," she said, hating the tears in her voice as well as on her cheeks. "Why weren't you here when I needed you?"

"You've never needed me."

Nicole watched him as he went back to her desk and made himself comfortable. "I won't discuss him. I told you before he's been dead for me for years. Now answer my question about Antoine. Why is he still here?"

"He's a very good cellarmaster. Invaluable to the winery." She sat on the sofa and dried her eyes once more.

Lalo closed the ledger and put it away in the desk drawer. It irritated her the way he made himself so comfortable in her home. This had always been Nicole's favorite room, used by her alone. Lalo never had any use for it, preferring an office in the winery during his brief attempt at running the business.

"How long are you staying?" she asked again. Her tone was sharp.

He leaned back in the chair and put his newly shined boots on the corner of her polished desk. "You don't sound glad to see me."

Her cheeks flushed with anger, and his laughter jolted her into remembering Antoine's words earlier when he had referred to Lalo as sick. That wasn't exactly news to her. Lalo drank too much and had a passion for recreational drugs. Any sickness he had was only a symptom of his real problems.

"The cook says that Eva's still here," he said boisterously. At the mention of Eva's name, the locked shutters across the room blew open and brought in an arctic gust of air. Lalo jumped up quickly and shut them, rubbing his arms to fight the chill. His eyes were huge, and his hands were visibly shaking. "I see the cook was right," he growled as he came back to the desk. The entire room was cold now, and the temperature seemed to be dropping even more.

"If I remember the family history correctly," Nicole said pointedly, "Eva had no one to protect her from her brother. Just how much like our grandfather would you like to be, Lalo?" They exchanged a look, with him glancing away first. "Have you come back to kill me?" she asked him calmly. "Choke the very life out of me? Install yourself as the Marquis? Take over the winery? Spend my money as frivolously as you've spent your own?"

"I would never hurt you, Nickie," he said in a voice full of emotion. "I love you. You're all the family I have left."

"Then you're here to stay?"

"Well, no."

"Then why did you come back? Is this just a friendly visit? I won't give you any money." She started to cry again, and Lalo came over to the sofa. "Look what you've done," she grumbled. "I hate to cry." He tried to put his arm around her, but she pushed him away. "Don't touch me," she said. He ignored her and pulled her closer to him. She cried on his shoulder as the temperature in the room continued to drop.

"I could never hurt you, Nickie. Please believe that."

She · dried her eyes again frantically. "What is it you want from me? You seem to have done rather well for yourself these last few years." His clothes were new and expensive, and the strange car parked at the winery was also new.

"I've met someone who likes taking care of me."

Nicole was not impressed. She was more concerned with Antoine's well-being than her brother's financial position. "What are your plans, Lalo? Are you here to help me with the winery? Winemaking always seemed to bore you." The room had grown so cold that their teeth began to chatter. Nicole tried to rub some warmth into her arms. "Go back to my desk. Eva doesn't like you being so close to me."

Lalo looked at her with wide eyes but returned to the chair behind the desk. It began to get warmer almost immediately, but there was still a lingering chill in the air. She noticed a trace of fear in his eyes that almost made her laugh.

"She's never liked me," he muttered. "Simon refuses to stay here. Last night was very unpleasant. Simon is my lover," he explained. "He's staying at the winery. Absolutely refuses to set foot in the château again."

Nicole couldn't have cared less about any discomfort he and his lover had experienced in the château. "Antoine is coming home tomorrow. What are your plans?" she asked again for what seemed like the hundredth time.

"He's not coming here," Lalo said indignantly. "I won't allow it."

Nicole's blue eyes narrowed as she glared at him. They were like children once more, bickering over everything they could, but Nicole was not going to give in to him this time. He would never again tell her what to do in her own home.

"*You* won't allow it?" she said slowly. "I don't recall anyone asking you. Antoine lives here. He works here. He's my friend, and I'm bringing him home. You have nothing to say about it. And another thing," she said as she pointed her finger at him, "I will *not* have you badgering the servants. Leave them alone. They aren't here for your convenience. And I've instructed them not to refer to you as the Marquis. I thought I made myself clear on that the last time you were here. You are *not*, and never have been, the Marquis. The title hasn't been used in eighty years. And another thing," she said, continuing to point her finger at him, "I won't have you bullying anyone even remotely connected with the château or the Jeton Vineyards. Things are much different from what they used to be."

"Don't push me, Nickie. I belong here, too. This is just as much my home as it is yours."

She ignored him. "What are your plans?" she asked him once more. She felt like he was still playing games with her. *What if he wants to bring his new lover here to live?* she wondered. *The château is large enough to accommodate everyone, but will Antoine stay if Lalo and his lover moves in with them?* The thought of losing Antoine upset her very much. Not only was he the best cellarmaster she had ever seen, he was also her best friend.

"I don't really have any plans," he said. His sandy-colored hair fell across his forehead as it always had. He was a stranger to her. *Whatever happened to the Lalo I loved as a child?* she wondered. *Where had he gone?*

"Who were you with this weekend?" he asked, his smile suddenly patronizing.

"A friend."

"Of course," he said. "I saw her leaving earlier. Not bad, I suppose, for a woman." He leaned back in the chair and smiled wickedly. "You're more of a man than I'll ever be. My sister the winemaster. The lover of women."

Nicole smiled also, receiving comfort in the knowledge that he resented her position. He had hurt her terribly the last time he was here. His games. His lack of maturity. He was a child at heart. Always needing the last laugh and enjoying the joke as long as it was at someone else's expense. The longer she watched him, the more she wanted him to leave. She had no guilt about these feelings, and it surprised her how little she felt for him.

He yanked open the desk drawer and took out the ledger. "I see that the winery has made a handsome profit since I've been away. You've done a good job, Nickie," he said. "You were right earlier. I think winemaking is boring. I have little or no interest in it at all, but," he said as he held the ledger up and waved it at her, "Jeton Vineyards is half mine. Half of everything you make belongs to me."

"You've spent your trust fund already, Lalo. You have no money here."

"I'm not talking about money, Nickie. I'm talking

about the vineyards. The profits you make from wine sales. Half of the vineyards are mine, so half of the profits should be mine as well."

"If you knew anything about business, Lalo, you would know that most of that money goes right back into the winery. The bankable profits are slim."

He loosened the red scarf around his neck as he leaned back in the chair. "Then I see only one feasible solution. You can buy me out. I'll sell you my half of the business."

Nicole was stunned. The winery had been in the family over a hundred years. What Jeton in his right mind would even *think* of selling it? "I have no idea what it's worth," she managed to say.

Lalo smiled. "We can have it appraised. It's only fair."

"Whatever the price is, Lalo, I'm sure I can't afford it. I don't have that kind of money."

"You have your trust fund," he reminded her. "You're my sister. We can work something out."

Nicole stared at him, feeling sad about what he had become. *He's found a way to get my money,* she thought. *He's probably planned this for years!* "What if I refuse to buy your half?"

"Then I'll find another buyer. You could work with a partner, couldn't you, Nickie?"

Camille called the château before leaving for work the next day, and Claudette informed her that Nicole had left for the hospital early. She took Camille's telephone number and promised to relay a message, but Camille doubted seriously that Nicole would return her call.

Late Monday evening, long after Camille had fallen asleep in her chair at home, Antoine called her. He was feeling much better but was uneasy about being at the château. He hadn't seen Lalo since his visit in the hospital.

"I'm sorry," Camille said sympathetically. "What happens now?"

"I don't know. I'm not sure what's going on here."

"How is Nicole?"

"Very distant," he said. "She hasn't said much. I'm glad she was gone when that idiot arrived. Thank you for at least saving her from that."

"Believe me, it was my pleasure," Camille said sincerely, remembering each and every time they had made love while they were away. "I know she doesn't want to see me, and I'm not sure what I'm going to do about that yet."

"I didn't realize there was a problem," he said. "That could explain why she's been so quiet."

"At this point I'm more inclined to believe that her moods are a result of her brother's presence than anything to do with me. She's made it clear that I've only imagined her feelings for me."

"I've known her a long time," Antoine said gently. "You've imagined nothing. Nicole can be very stubborn, but she cares for you. She tries to keep her emotions under control. If she's in love with you, I'm sure you'll be the last to know about it."

"A comforting thought," Camille said. "I have a habit of falling in love with complicated women. I

95

feel like such a fool, Antoine. I don't believe I'll be calling again."

"Don't give up. Let me talk to her. I'll be in touch."

Chapter Ten

The May sunshine slowly warmed them as they rode to the vineyards. Antoine walked the rows with her, randomly checking the vines and watching Nicole as she scribbled in her notebook.

"You've been very quiet lately," he commented. "Is Lalo still upsetting you?"

"Upsetting me?" He's trying to *ruin* me, she wanted to say, but divulging her financial situation to him now would only embarrass her. Nicole wasn't ready to talk about any of this yet. "It's nothing that you need to worry about," she said after a moment.

"He seems to be keeping a very low profile."

"Yes. That's the least he could do under the circumstances."

They strolled on, kneeling occasionally to inspect the roots and take a few soil samples, only to rise and dust themselves off before continuing down the row.

"I talked to Camille yesterday," Antoine said. "She seems a little confused."

"I suppose she is," Nicole said almost in a whisper. "I wouldn't blame her if she never spoke to me again."

"Did something happen on your trip together?"

"Oh, yes," Nicole sighed, "something happened. Something wonderful happened." Even to Antoine she couldn't say the words out loud. She felt all tied up inside, a bundle of emotion unlike anything she had ever experienced before, as if vocalizing her true feelings would somehow only complicate her life further. "If I've lost her, then maybe it's for the best."

"Is that what you want?"

"For now," she said as they stopped walking. They looked at each other for the first time all day. His dark wavy hair was scrambled from the wind, and the small bandage on his forehead seemed extraordinarily white against his tanned face. "Everything I've done, Antoine, I've had to do. She's the most wonderful person I've ever known. She loves me. I knew that the first time she touched me."

"You love her also," he said with a smile. "You're not being fair to her, Nicole. Tell her how you feel. It's not too late. It's never too late."

"This is a bad time. I can't deal with her *and*

Lalo. I need all my strength for him without any distractions."

"Forget about Lalo. Think of yourself for once. Where will you ever find another Camille?"

She didn't answer him because she knew there was no answer. He was right, but how could she tell him what she was up against? If Lalo got his way and sold his share of the winery to someone else, they could all be looking for new jobs. What if the partner wanted to bring in employees of his own? What if he's a winemaster, too? Or even a cellarmaster? She and Antoine worked so well together. The thought of strangers in her winery and in her vineyards almost made her shudder. She couldn't allow it to happen. Her only alternative was to give Lalo her money in exchange for his share of the vineyards. Even though Nicole had never had much use for a lot of money, and certainly had no time to spend any of it, her financial security had at least given her the freedom to be the kind of winemaker she wanted to be. Nicole had never considered any of this a job before, only something her family had always done because they loved doing it. Being a successful winemaker now took on an entirely new meaning. Winemaking would become survival.

"We're finished here," she said, and turned toward her horse leisurely munching grass. Their whole lives were about to change, and Nicole didn't handle change well.

Marguerite kept in touch, spreading various

degrees of cheer and discontent. Camille's birthday was close, and Marguerite was all for throwing a lavish party for her favorite cousin. Camille did what she could to discourage the idea, but as usual she was far from successful.

"It'll be *fun!*" Marguerite squealed excitedly. "I'm even having Monique and Gaston pick you up so you can't slip out on me again. I've got a carnival of activity planned for you." Marguerite was determined, and Camille could see no way out. "Tomorrow at seven. Be ready."

Camille had forgotten all about her birthday. Where had the year gone? Birthdays were bad enough in their own right, but the thought of a birthday party at Marguerite's depressed her even more.

Camille went to work early and was pleasantly surprised that her secretary remembered the day as well. Her boss took her to lunch and highly complimented her on her work, but again without the benefit of a raise. Camille had no idea why he liked her so much. She didn't believe she worked any harder than anyone else on the staff.

She went home early to get ready for the party. Her sister, Monique, a slightly plumper version of Camille, and brother-in-law, Gaston, were to pick her up and escort her to Marguerite's for the festivities. Camille smiled as she put on her earrings and glanced at the clock when she heard the knock on her apartment door.

"Come in," she said as Monique and Gaston swept in.

"Happy birthday, Camille," Gaston said as he kissed her cheek. "You look marvelous."

"Yes, you do," Monique affirmed.

"Make yourself comfortable. I'm not ready yet."
Camille hurried into her bedroom to put on the
finishing touches.

In the library at the château, Nicole was going
over invoices and trying hard not to think about
Camille. Marguerite had called the day before to
invite her to the party, but Nicole had declined.
Making arrangements for the upcoming sale of a good
portion of their five-year-old vintage as well as
worrying about Lalo's latest antics kept her too busy
to think about Camille most of the time. She had
started to call her on several occasions during the
last few days but had talked herself out of it. *Why
not now?* she wondered. With determination Nicole
put down the stack of papers and reached for the
telephone. She dialed the number and hesitated when
another woman answered.

"Camille Cartier, please," Nicole said uneasily,
hoping she had the wrong number.

"One moment."

Nicole fought the urge to hang up. *Have I sent
her away into another woman's arms already?* she
wondered. The thought unsettled her a little.

"Hello," came Camille's voice.

"This is Nicole," she managed to say. "Have I
called at a bad time?"

"No, of course not," Camille said, her voice
suddenly softer. "I wasn't sure I would hear from
you again."

The sound of the woman's voice still echoed in
Nicole's head. She had to force herself not to ask

who the woman was. "How are things with your brother?" she heard Camille ask.

"He's being difficult. Antoine is feeling much better, though." There was silence as they both seemed to take this opportunity to breathe a little easier. "Happy birthday," Nicole said.

"Thank you."

More silence. Nicole knew Camille wouldn't let her out of this easily. "Be patient with me, Camille."

"You're leaving me no choice. I want to see you again, Nicole, but that doesn't seem to be what you want." More silence followed. It was very unnerving. "I hope everything works out for you."

Hearing the resignation and defeat as Camille spoke made Nicole want to hold her and make everything right again. She was handling this badly, but didn't know what else to do. Thoughts of the woman who had answered Camille's telephone popped in and out of her mind as she imagined all sorts of things. She couldn't believe how things had gotten in such a mess so quickly.

"I'm not very good at this," Nicole said finally. The right words had escaped her.

"Good at what? Discouraging an unwanted lover once you're finished with her?"

"Camille!"

"So tell me what happens after things settle down there."

Nicole nervously tapped her fingers on her desk and forced herself not to cry. "I'm not very good at this," she whispered again, knowing if she told Camille how much she loved her, Camille would probably arrive before the night was over.

"I can make this easy for you, Nicole, but I'm not

sure I want to. I can honestly say it's been fun and you've given me the most wonderful three weeks of my life. I'm sorry things didn't work out."

Nicole snapped the pencil she had been using and dropped the two pieces on the desk. Camille's tone frightened her. "I care enough about you to want to keep you in Paris right now," Nicole said.

"You care enough about me?" Camille repeated. "And what exactly does that mean? Remember, Nicole. You need to be careful what you say to someone who can so easily mistake sex for love. I've always been immature in that respect."

"Camille," she whispered tiredly. "Please. Must you believe everything I tell you?"

Camille's sudden laughter was a surprise. Nicole held the telephone tightly, knowing exactly what was expected of her. This was where she had to confess the love that was filling her heart. This was where she should explain her fears of poverty to the only person in the world who mattered any longer. They were such easy words on the surface. Nothing complicated. Nothing unreasonable. Nicole rubbed her eyes. She was getting a headache. A winemaster must learn to take chances early, she reminded herself. Just say, I love you enough to want to keep you away right now. Easy words. Nothing complicated. The memory of another woman answering Camille's telephone nagged her. Nicole imagined the woman to be beautiful and possibly even an old lover. It was too soon for Camille to have a new lover already. She was certain of that. Nicole took a deep breath.

"Happy birthday," was all she could say. And they were hard words. Very complicated.

"Thank you," Camille said and hung up.

* * * * *

Camille was depressed when she joined her sister and brother-in-law in the hallway. They were waiting with their raincoats on, ready to go. She had taken a few minutes to freshen her makeup and regain her composure; she had made a few decisions of her own during those last few moments alone. *A relationship takes work on both parts,* she thought. *I've given all I can give. The next move has to be hers. Absolutely no more calls from me or trips to Burgundy. Nicole has to want this to happen too,* Camille decided.

"Who was that?" Monique asked with a smirk. She knew her sister was a lesbian, and she had a curiosity that could only rival their cousin Marguerite's.

"A friend," Camille said as they left. "It's my birthday, you know."

"Yes, we know," Gaston said as he opened another door for them and glanced at his watch. They were late.

Chapter Eleven

The same string quartet was there playing to an uninterested crowd, while family and friends that Camille hadn't seen in ages arrived in droves. Camille noticed that Marguerite's husband had not missed the opportunity to invite some of his clients. The sight of a few of those familiar faces made her smile as she recalled meeting Nicole that evening.

Camille spent a good deal of time going from person to person and making small talk as she slowly swirled, sniffed, and sipped her champagne. Near the veranda Camille spied a small tentlike structure made of multicolored veils. A light shone from inside the tent, and silhouettes of guests could be seen through the flimsy scarves. Camille watched as she maneuvered around a group and saw a line of happy party-goers forming in front of the tent. It was all quite bizarre looking.

"What do you think?" Marguerite asked as she slipped up behind her.

"You've outdone yourself," Camille said and hugged her. "This is the best birthday party I've ever had."

Marguerite puffed on her cigarette and took a sip of champagne. "How was the villa?" she asked with a gleam in her eye.

"Wonderful. Thank you for letting us use it."

"It never occurred to me how much you and Nicole had in common."

Monique, who was not quite so tall as her sister, joined them with a glass of champagne in each hand. "Camille, have you had your palm read?"

Marguerite touched Camille's shoulder. "Have you been to see the fortune-teller I got for your party? You know how I'm always looking for new types of entertainment." Camille's puzzled expression told them all they needed to know.

Marguerite and Monique cleared a path among the guests and escorted the birthday girl to the head of the line in front of the tent. Marguerite parted the pink and yellow veils just in time for one of the guests to come out. The gypsy was free. Marguerite poked her head inside and announced that the guest of honor would be next.

"Camille, dear. Come here."

The string quartet played softly in the

background, and the guests in line encouraged Camille to go in. She felt extremely self-conscious knowing all eyes were on her, but she went forward and peered inside. There were a small table, two chairs, and a bright light sitting on an apple crate in the corner. The tent itself was small but colorful.

The gypsy was young, maybe in her late twenties, with long black hair, olive-colored skin, and dark, piercing eyes. She was serious, but pleasant, and motioned for Camille to sit across from her.

"The crystal ball," Marguerite said excitedly. "She wants the crystal ball. It's much more fun."

Camille turned to Marguerite, who was standing in the doorway, and said, "I don't think I want to do this."

"Of *course* you do! You'll love it."

Camille rolled her eyes, passed her champagne glass to her cousin, and nudged her outside. "It's my future," she said. "At least give me some privacy." She turned back around and met the gypsy's eyes. "I don't think I want to do this," she said again.

"It's harmless," the gypsy said reassuringly. Her French had a strange accent that Camille had never heard before. "Please, sit down." Camille arranged her dress nervously as the faint smell of wood smoke drifted toward her from across the table. "Shall we do the crystal ball first?"

"Sure," Camille said with a shrug.

The gypsy uncovered the glowing sphere in the middle of the table and stared into it mysteriously. Her dark hands were folded neatly in front of her as a smile played at the corner of her mouth. She was pretty in an exotic sort of way, with black eyes that flickered in the crystal ball's light.

"I see someone for you," the gypsy said. She raised her eyes with only the very beginnings of a smile on her lips. "She's quite beautiful."

Camille gaped at her as the thought of Nicole came to mind. She felt herself blushing, having this stranger know so much about her personal life already.

"You've known passion. You will know it again. But I see danger for you," she said. "Danger for her also. You are both surrounded by evil." The gypsy jumped back quickly with wide and frightened eyes. When the gypsy jumped, Camille jumped also. "There is a man," she said, "a tall, handsome man. He's very dangerous."

"What does he look like?" Camille demanded as her skin began to tingle. She was certain it was Lalo.

"Stay away," the gypsy warned again, almost in a trance. Her eyes opened wider as she stared.

"Now what? What exactly do you see in there?" Camille demanded again.

The gypsy quickly threw a scarf over the crystal ball. "I'm sorry. I can't help you."

Camille leaned forward and grabbed her arm. "I'm afraid you'll have to do better than that. Now tell me what you saw."

"Next!" the gypsy said loudly as she pulled at the scarves dangling beside her that posed as a flimsy door. "Someone else wish to have their fortune told?" she called to those waiting outside.

The man with the bald spot came in with a turquoise veil draped over his shoulder. Camille shot him a look that stopped him cold. "We're not quite finished here yet," she said. "It's my birthday. I need more time." He backed out slowly and Camille stood up, towering over the woman.

"What do you know about Nicole? What kind of evil did you see?" she asked with determination in her voice. "Tell me everything."

"I can't help you," the gypsy snapped.

Camille heard fear in her voice. "You saw something," she said, trying to stay calm. "Tell me what you know."

"Evil. That's all I know." The gypsy moved her hand frantically among the scarves beside her, wanting a new customer desperately.

"Death? Ghosts? What?" she asked excitedly as she yanked the woman away from the door. "Tell me!" *Gypsies and crystal balls,* she thought to herself. *What's the matter with me?* she wondered as she eyed the woman more closely. *Do I really believe in this?*

Camille made her way through the scarves and out of the tent. Marguerite and Monique were waiting for her. Marguerite handed her a fresh glass of champagne, and Camille gulped it quickly without benefit of sniffing or swirling.

"What's in your future?" her sister asked.

"Isn't this fun?" Marguerite chirped.

"Yes," Camille said, her mind clicking away as she smiled and nodded. "Very informative."

"What did she tell you?" Monique insisted.

Camille smiled at her sister and said, "There's a beautiful woman in my future."

Marguerite squeezed her shoulder fondly. "Spare us the details."

Camille let her eyes drift back to the gypsy's tent every now and then as the participants continued to line up for their peek at the future, while well-wishers and new arrivals continued to shower her with compliments.

Camille was informed that she had a telephone call, and she excused herself from the cluster of people around her. Nearly everyone she knew was already in attendance, so who would possibly be calling her? She took the telephone into a coat closet that offered the only sliver of privacy anywhere in the house and was much quieter. As she leaned against a fur coat, she cracked the door to let in some light and a bit of fresh air.

"Hello."

"Camille," came that wonderful voice that could make her weak all over. It was Nicole, sounding small and upset. "Forgive me for interrupting your party, but I can't stop thinking about you."

Camille felt the warmth rush through her as the words registered quickly. She sank even farther into the fur, oblivious to its effect on her allergies. "Nicole," she said.

"I just wanted to hear your voice again. Have I made a terrible mess of things? Don't answer," Nicole said quickly. "I know I have."

Thoughts of the gypsy came to Camille, and the insistent warning of prevailing evil surrounding them made her snap to attention.

"You're in danger, Nicole. I know it. I can feel it." She didn't have the nerve to say a gypsy had told her so.

"Danger? Don't be silly. Everything is fine here.

That woman in your apartment earlier," Nicole said sheepishly, "who was she?"

Camille listened closely, but didn't quite connect with the question for a moment. She was still in shock at hearing from Nicole again so soon. Camille smiled as she remembered Nicole's confession of being so possessive. *Could she be jealous?* Camille mused. *How wonderfully juvenile.* "That was Monique." The words *my sister* would not pass through her lips. Not yet anyway. Nicole had to make the next move. "Monique and I came to the party together."

"I see," Nicole said crisply. "How long have you known her?"

"All my life. We're very close." It was not like Camille to play these adolescent games, but she felt as though Nicole had brought it all on herself. As she stood there among the various assortment of raincoats and furs, the word *evil* again stayed fresh in her mind, amplifying itself as she touched the door. Nicole was in danger. Evil could mean so many things. *It could even be Eva,* she thought suddenly. *Aren't ghosts and spirits evil?*

"How is Eva?" Camille asked urgently.

"Eva is fine. It's quiet here now. She's restless when Lalo is around, so he stays at the winery with his new friend."

Maybe Lalo was the evil the gypsy had referred to, Camille reasoned. She claimed to have seen a tall, handsome man in the crystal ball. Camille rolled her eyes. *Am I really believing this?* she wondered. Somehow it just seemed silly to take chances.

"You're in danger, Nicole. I'll be out of town tomorrow, but I'll call you. Please be careful."

111

"Where are you going?" Nicole demanded. "Camille," she said desperately, "please. Who is this Monique person? Are you going away with her?"

Camille felt lightheaded as she listened. The desperation in Nicole's voice registered plainly and gave her hope. "I refuse to make this easy for you, Nicole. I've made a fool of myself over you, but then love tends to make me do that sort of thing."

"I called to tell you how very important you are to me."

"Important," Camille repeated. "Will you ever be able to tell me that you love me, Nicole? Or maybe I should ask if you'll ever be able to love me? Which is it?"

"Camille," she whispered. There was a long pause. Finally Nicole said, "I've spoiled your birthday. I'm sorry. I don't even know why I called."

"You wanted to know who the woman in my apartment was," Camille reminded her dryly. "Monique is my sister. Maybe I failed to mention that."

"Your sister," Nicole said. "You were quite aware of what I wanted to know!"

"Yes," Camille said, "quite aware. There were even a few moments when I believed you might be jealous, but once again I was obviously mistaken. I'm not sure I'll ever understand you, Nicole. You claim to be very possessive, but what exactly does that mean? You'd have to care about something in order to want to possess it."

"I do care —"

"I'm not a toy you can take out and play with when the mood strikes you, Nicole. I have feelings. I want to help you."

"I'll call you after I take care of my brother," Nicole said angrily. "We'll talk about this then!"

Camille hung up the telephone and struggled out of the coat closet. She wanted to have another word with that gypsy before she left.

Chapter Twelve

Nicole slept terribly and was even more irritable the following morning. She stormed to the winery and barked a few orders to the staff. Lalo and his lover were in her office when she arrived, which didn't please her either.

Lalo stood up when she came in. She felt her anger growing even more at the sight of him. He was wearing an exact replica of the outfit their grandfather had worn when his portrait had been painted. The two of them looked so much alike that

Nicole found herself backing up a few steps away from him.

"Where did you get those clothes?" she finally managed to ask.

"I had them made. You like it?" He strutted around her office showing off his costume. "This is Simon Jonas, by the way. I don't believe you two have met."

Nicole shook his hand. *So, this is the twit,* she thought as she remembered the word Antoine had used for him. He was younger than she expected, with short, neat blond hair and a stocky muscular build. The blond mustache was wasted on him. It blended right in with his pale complexion. *Not Lalo's usual type,* she thought.

"I'm Nicole Jeton."

"I've heard a lot about you from your brother." His French was excellent, but he was not a Frenchman. Possibly he was an American.

"Your French is very good."

Simon smiled at the compliment. "Thank you." He had a twinkle in his eye as he glanced at Lalo. "It's gotten much better during the last year."

"Simon is from the United States," Lalo offered. "We met in California."

"I see," Nicole said, moving to her desk. She nudged him out of the way with her elbow as she selected a notebook from the drawer. She collected a few things and went to the door.

"Where are you off to, Nickie?" he asked, referring to her riding clothes.

"To check the vineyards. We've had a lot of rain. While you've been playing, Lalo, I've had to wade in

115

the mud and fight gray rot on the crop. You probably don't even know what gray rot looks like, do you?" She slammed the door and descended the stairs two at a time, slapping the notebook against her thigh.

Antoine had their horses waiting outside and held the reins as Nicole climbed up into the saddle. An even smaller bandage replaced the one he had worn the day before. His color was back to normal, and Nicole was close to letting him resume his regular duties at the winery.

"Wait until you see what Lalo is wearing today," she said.

"The pink chiffon again?" Antoine asked dryly. Their laughter carried all the way to the river.

Nicole took the end of one vineyard while Antoine took the other. They tied their horses and walked the rows, checking and inspecting the vines. Nicole jotted down several notes and took a few more soil samples. Her boots and riding clothes were soon caked with mud. Everything looked good. The new pesticide seemed to be helping tremendously.

Nicole glanced up as she heard a car door and saw Lalo coming down the ridge in his new Marquis suit. The sight of him still affected her strangely. He had changed so much from the Lalo she remembered. He was greedier and much lazier. Still she couldn't help but love him. No matter what he did, he was still her brother. They had played together, grown up together, and at one time had briefly worked together. Now she saw him as a threat to her happiness and very livelihood.

"Any sign of gray rot?" he called to her as he trotted down the hill. Nicole smiled as she noticed that he stayed on the grass. Getting mud on his new suit would never do.

"What are you doing down here?"

"I have to talk to you," he said. "Simon is anxious. He wants to get back to California."

Nicole slowly worked her way down the row toward him.

"He doesn't like sleeping in the winery and hates being so close to what he refers to as a haunted château. How long has Eva been doing this?"

"It started a few days before Papa died," she said. "It started up again just before you arrived. Your friend could get a good night's sleep in the château, Lalo. He's not the one Eva objects to." His confused expression made her chuckle. "It's you Eva dislikes. How do you expect her to react when you dress like Philippe and insist upon being referred to as the Marquis? You're so much like the man who murdered her, I'm surprised something dreadful hasn't happened to you. Take my advice, Lalo. Let Simon sleep at the château, and you sleep at the winery."

"Your explanation seems a bit farfetched," he said. Nicole was standing next to him. Lalo towered over her by almost a foot. "Have you thought about my offer, Nickie? I can find another buyer for my half of the vineyard. I don't have much time."

"Why the rush?"

He kicked at a clump of grass with his shiny new boot. "We have a chance to invest in a winery in California. I need the money."

"My money," she reminded him.

"Your money?" he said. "When Papa died

everything should have been left to me, Nicole. Jeton women have never owned anything. All of this," he said as he waved his arms, "should belong to me. The Marquis owns everything!"

She untied her horse and put the test tubes and notebook carefully in a saddlebag. She looked down at him from her horse and could only shake her head.

"I'll need your decision by this evening," he said as he stared up at her. "Consider yourself lucky that I haven't asked for my share of what the château is worth. Half of that belongs to me also."

"You'll probably be back in three years with your hand out again. I figure it will take you about that long to spend what you've managed to get out of me this time. You're despicable, Lalo."

"You know I'm right," he said triumphantly.

"I've made it work," she said as she leaned toward him on the horse. Nicole was so angry she could hardly speak. "And you want to take *my* money and invest in a winery in California? Not two days ago you told me how much you hated this business. Never had any interest in it!"

Lalo stood up straighter and squared his shoulders. "You should have seen how they treated me, Nickie. They heard my name and asked if I knew of the Jeton Vineyards of Dijon. You should have seen their faces when I said I *was* the Jeton from Dijon. They treated me better than royalty. My name alone will make me a fortune in America."

"You're a fool, Lalo," she said, turning her horse around.

"I'll need your decision by this evening!" he yelled after her.

Antoine caught up with her at the river. They

rode along together in silence, him not asking questions, and her hoping he wouldn't. They dismounted and walked for a while, their horses nibbling at grass as she and Antoine watched the river.

"Camille and I made love under this tree," she said finally. Sharing something so intimate with him seemed important to her for some reason.

Antoine smiled and pointed to a tree about fifteen feet away in the other direction. "Lalo and I preferred that one." They laughed and hugged each other. "Have you settled things with her yet?"

"I'm afraid I've made matters worse than they were before. She's wonderful, Antoine. So open. So honest. So beautiful." Nicole smiled at the thought of Camille. "She makes me laugh. I don't laugh much anymore."

"That's true," he said, "but then we haven't had much to laugh about the last few years, have we?"

"We've managed," she said, touching his arm fondly. They began walking again, leading the horses. "He's going to the United States. To California to make wine."

"Be serious, Nicole," Antoine chuckled. "Lalo was never happy making wine, although there was a time when he was quite good at it. Not as good as you are. That always bothered him. He's been jealous of you for years. Claiming to be uninterested in wine was a way out for him. A way to keep from admitting that you were better at it. His heritage. His life. After all, Philippe was a great winemaster, wasn't he?"

Nicole listened and began to see her brother a little differently through Antoine's eyes. Lalo was going to a place where his name was important. He would finally have the respect he felt he deserved. Here at the Jeton Vineyards he would never be more than a second-rate winemaster. In California he would be a genius.

"He knows much more about winemaking than I give him credit for," she said. She felt bad about accusing him of not being able to recognize gray rot. "Before he started gambling and drinking, he was an asset to us, Antoine. The year before he left I remember as being our worst. He was more of a hindrance than anything." She sighed. "How can he be a winemaster? He'll taste the profits away."

They walked on in silence, each lost in the memory of the Lalo they both used to know.

Chapter Thirteen

Nicole was hard at work in the lab at the winery, running tests on the soil samples and going over another pesticide she had considered using on the crop, when the telephone rang in her office. Her heart raced for a moment, thinking it might be Camille. She emptied her hands and hurried across the hall, but the telephone stopped ringing before she could get to it.

She closed the lab and went back to the château. She had put off facing Lalo long enough. She went straight to the library where she knew he would be waiting for her. She opened the door and found him with a glass of wine in one hand and a nearly empty bottle in the other. His feet were again propped up on the corner of her desk.

"I was about to come after you," he said. His speech was slurred as he smiled at her. "I should have known you wouldn't forget. My little Nickie never forgets anything. What's your answer? Will you buy me out?"

"When did you start drinking again?"

Lalo giggled. "About an hour ago."

"In California, Lalo," she said as she came to the end of the sofa, "what exactly do you expect to do at an American winery?"

"I'll be a consultant. Something important. Buying equipment. Planting grapes. Inspecting. What is your answer, Nickie? Do you want Jeton Vineyards to yourself, or will you need a partner of my choosing?"

There was a knock on the library door as Claudette came in shyly carrying a service of coffee. Nicole hated the way Lalo intimidated the servants.

"I ordered us refreshments," he said.

"If you're staying here you'll stop drinking," Nicole said. "You're a disgrace."

He smiled at her stupidly. She moved to the side of the desk and gave his boots a shove. His feet hit the floor sharply, causing the wine in his glass to slosh on him. There was a deeply buried anger inside of her that had been brewing for a long time. She wanted an end to his smugness, his arrogance, and his threats to destroy her.

"I want you sober when we talk, Lalo," she said coldly. "I'll let you know my decision tomorrow." Nicole took what was left of the wine with her, leaving him with only the coffee. On her way down the hall she heard Antoine's laughter from the foyer. He and Simon were coming in together. She stopped and watched them, surprised at how well they seemed to be getting along.

Simon smiled his young, toothy smile. "Do you know where Lalo is?" he asked.

"In the library. He's been drinking."

The smile left his face as he started towards the library. It was obvious that a drunken Lalo was nothing new to him either. Nicole and Antoine went to the drawing room where Antoine poured them each a glass of wine. She rested her head on the back of the sofa and gazed up at Eva's portrait.

"How long are you going to wait before you tell me what Lalo is up to?" Antoine asked from the chair beside her.

She slowly cut her eyes over at him and swirled the contents of her glass. "You needn't worry about him. I can handle my brother."

"Simon tells me Lalo is here to claim his inheritance. Has he asked you for money?"

Nicole closed her tired eyes and tugged at her muddy boot with the other foot. Antoine stood to help her remove them. "So now suddenly he's 'Simon' instead of 'the twit,'" she said with an impish grin. "Could that possibly be the reason Lalo is falling down drunk in the library? What exactly have you and Simon been doing?"

Antoine set the muddy boots in the hallway and dusted himself off before returning to his chair and wine glass.

"I may have misjudged the twit," he said. "Lalo has apparently cast his usual spell over the young

123

man. You have cleverly changed the subject, I've noticed. Please, Nicole. Tell me what's happening. Maybe I can help."

She sighed and let him take her glass. "He wants to sell his portion of Jeton Vineyards. Whether it's to me or anyone else, he doesn't care. I have until tomorrow to give him my answer. Either my inheritance in exchange for his share of the winery, or else he'll sell to someone else and force me into a partnership. Either way I lose, Antoine. You and I will both lose."

"I had no idea," he whispered.

Nicole smiled bitterly. "He's actually doing me a favor, I'm sure, by offering to trade my inheritance for his share of the vineyard. If he were to sell to someone else he could get much more. Neither one of us knows what the winery is actually worth, but I'm certain that what I have would hardly come close." A tear rolled down her cheek as she gazed at Eva's portrait again. "I'll never understand him. And I'll never forgive him for this."

Antoine emptied his glass and refilled it once again. "Have you made up your mind?"

"Of course I've made up my mind," Nicole said. "I'll give him the money. I can't let strangers come in here telling us what to do. There will have to be some changes, though. Winemaking takes on a whole new meaning for me now. It's survival. The fun will be gone and the pressure will be on." She smiled at him tiredly. "No more late harvests."

He laughed. "You'll always gamble. I've never seen instincts like yours. It might be rough the first couple of years, but we've always had successful crops, Nicole."

"I know," she said uneasily. "And we're overdue for a bad one. The odds are against us. Will it be this year? Next year? The year after? No rain? Too much rain? I'll have nothing to fall back on. A bad crop could ruin us. Damn him! How can he do this to me?"

"You talk as if the winery never makes a profit on its own, Nicole. You're bound to be making money off of it."

"Our equipment is old. We've replaced some of it during the last couple of years. We've enlarged the vat room and installed new heating in the nursery. What will we need next year, Antoine? And the year after? We show a sizable profit every year, but I'm putting everything right back into the winery. It takes money to make money." She looked at him wearily and nodded. "Don't worry. We'll do fine. I have an appointment with my lawyer in the morning. I'm tired. I'm going to bed."

Antoine walked with her to the stairs where they found Claudette.

"Wake me at seven," Nicole told her. "And I'm not in for anyone except Mademoiselle Cartier."

"Are you expecting a call from Camille?" he asked her with a grin.

"No, but if she were to call I certainly wouldn't want to miss it."

"I see. Good night then."

Camille was reading in her chair when Antoine called. It was good to hear his voice.

"Were you asleep?" he asked with concern.

"Goodness no. How are you?"

"I'm fine. I have news about Nicole that I'm sure you will be interested in."

Camille set the manuscript down and took off her glasses. He had her undivided attention. "How is she, Antoine? I can't believe things have turned out this way for us."

"She's under a lot of strain right now. Lalo apparently is forcing her to buy his share of the vineyard. That's why she's been so upset. I want you to come for a visit. Can you get away?"

"She's told me quite bluntly that she doesn't want to see me," Camille said. "I don't think it's a good idea. I have no intention of being anywhere I'm not wanted."

"Nicole needs you now. She needs both of us. I can't do it all alone."

Camille arranged to take the remainder of the week off, packed a few things, and was on her way to Burgundy the following morning. She was to be Antoine's guest, should anyone dare question her presence at the château. She had no idea what he had planned for her.

She sped up the long driveway, more nervous on this occasion than she had been either of the other times she had come. The thought of seeing Nicole again both excited and depressed her. *If she makes a scene or asks me to leave I'll never come back,* she promised herself. How much humiliation can one person be expected to take?

She parked her car and knocked on the huge wooden door. Claudette answered with a smile and let her in quickly. The maid placed a call to the winery, and a few minutes later Antoine came in carrying her luggage.

"Camille," he said warmly as he gave her a hug. "I'll show you to your room."

They climbed the stairs, and Antoine led the way to the same room she had been in her first night there. "Nicole is with her lawyer this morning. She should be back any time. What would you like to do? Come over to the winery with me? Go for a ride? Stay here and rest for a while?"

"What would you like for me to do?" She still wasn't sure why she was there. He had given her the impression that she could be of help to Nicole, but Camille felt nothing but uneasiness at the prospect of seeing her again.

He laughed pleasantly. "That's entirely up to you. I have to get back over there. I have a tour that should be arriving soon. You haven't taken my tour yet. It's much better than Nicole's. After that I'll be free for a while and I'll be able to catch you up on things."

"Then I'll be over there shortly."

After he left, Camille sat on the edge of the huge bed and kicked her shoes off. She enjoyed being at the château. Later she would insist on a more thorough tour of it. She freshened her makeup and arrived at the winery just as the tour bus drove up. If nothing else, Marguerite's ghastly parties had at least taught her how to mingle.

* * * * *

Nicole arranged to meet Lalo in her office at the winery later that afternoon. He had been sick with a hangover most of the day.

"You know you shouldn't drink," she reminded him as she sat behind her desk. There was a cool breeze blowing in through the window behind her.

"Don't lecture me," he grumbled.

"Why do you do it?"

"Maybe I like it," he snapped. "Maybe I like feeling this way." He straightened the bright red scarf around his neck and stretched his long legs out in front of him. "Have you made a decision?"

"Yes," she said, staring at him. "My lawyer is drawing up the papers today. They should be ready tomorrow. I have one stipulation, however." His chuckle grated on her nerves unmercifully. "When you sign over your share of the winery to me, you will also forfeit all rights to the château."

"Do you really think that's fair?"

"As fair as your ending up with the entire family fortune," she retorted. "That's my stipulation. I plan to grow old here, Lalo. I like knowing I'll always have a place to live. A place that you can't take away from me."

"Then I'll need more money. The château is probably worth as much as the winery."

"Probably," she agreed. "I have no idea how much any of it's worth. I'm under the impression that you and Simon are anxious to get back to California. You can be on your way tomorrow evening," she said, fighting to keep her voice calm, "or you can stay here as long as you like and try to sell your half of the vineyards on your own." She knew what his answer would be even before making the offer. His greed showed through him like ribs on a skeleton. Selling the winery on his own would be too much like work.

"On my way to California by tomorrow evening," he repeated with a smile. "I see no reason why we can't keep Jeton Vineyards in the Jeton family. And consider my half of the château as a gift, Nicole. A gift for all the grief you say I've caused you." His broad smile almost made her sick. After he signed the papers tomorrow, she never wanted to see him again. "Let's all have dinner together this evening. A celebration."

"I think not, Lalo," she said. "The less time we spend together now, the better."

Camille and Antoine spent the afternoon riding near the river and looking over the vineyard. They talked about Lalo and Nicole and their own precarious love lives. No one had mentioned Camille's arrival. Too much had been going on for anyone to notice her car in the drive.

As Antoine and Camille sipped their wine in the drawing room later that evening, Claudette announced that the Marquis wanted dinner at eight and everyone was to be present.

"He loves pretending that he's royalty," Antoine explained to Camille. "It drives Nicole crazy."

Camille gazed up at Eva's portrait over the fireplace, and had trouble keeping her eyes off of it. "She's beautiful," she said.

"Eva? Yes, indeed. An interesting woman even now. I do wish that her poor soul could be laid to rest."

It began to thunder and the lights flickered. The rain pounded the window as Camille continued to try to absorb the entire personality of the portrait. Those eyes were Nicole's eyes, and that wonderful smile was Nicole's smile.

"It looks as though we'll be dining with the Marquis," Camille said as she swirled the wine in her glass. "I've never met him."

"Really?" Antoine said. "You'll either like him or despise him. Depends on how he feels at the moment. He seems to be in a festive mood because of Nicole's defeat. I think he'll try to win you over."

"I'm afraid he'll have to try very hard." She watched Antoine cross the room and peek through the drapes before coming back to his chair. "How late does she usually work?" Camille asked.

"Nine or ten. Sometimes later."

They heard the front door slam as a burst of deep male laughter filled the foyer, accompanied by a great deal of stomping and brushing sounds. Moments later Lalo and Simon came into the room and stopped abruptly. Simon poured himself a drink and lifted his glass to Antoine.

"Lalo Jeton and Simon Jonas, this is Camille Cartier. She'll be staying with us for a few days."

Lalo came around the sofa to shake her hand. He was as tall as she imagined him to be, and much more handsome than the picture she had seen of him. *So this is the man who is making my life miserable,* she thought.

"Nice meeting both of you," she said pleasantly as he continued to hold her hand.

Lalo smiled and nodded. "The pleasure is mine," he said with an amused expression. "Aren't you the one who sleeps with my sister?"

Camille retrieved her hand and felt her cheeks blush crimson. "Every chance I get," she replied.

Nicole transcribed her daily notes into the journal for the current crop. She kept busy ridding her desk of all paperwork; she liked starting each day free of the previous day's activity. Tomorrow would be a symbolic day of sorts. Jeton Vineyards would actually be hers and hers alone. Suddenly it didn't matter that she had considered it hers all along. That had only been a misconception on her part all of those years, but tomorrow it would really belong to her. It gave her a sense of pride knowing she had sacrificed something for the winery. No other Jeton had ever had to do such a thing. She stood alone in that respect, a notch above the rest of the family in her love for the vineyards. Above all else, the winery had to come first.

She kept her thoughts of Lalo to a minimum, but she found herself almost smiling as she recalled him in the vineyard in his Marquis outfit, dodging the mud and strutting around for the world to see. *How different we are,* she thought, *yet raised by the same man and given the same opportunities, even the same values.*

There were times when she wanted a peek at the

past just to see what kind of man her grandfather had been. How much alike were he and Lalo? Philippe had surely never suffered from greed or laziness as profusely as Lalo. He had helped build the family fortune and harvested some of the first grapes. Nicole had the suspicion that Lalo and Philippe Jeton had very little in common at all other than their physical appearance.

When she finished the paperwork and turned off the light, it was nearly ten-thirty. She was tired and emotionally drained from the continuous bickering with Lalo. She checked all doors and windows inside and locked everything up. The rain had stopped. She tried dodging puddles as best she could, but her boots and riding clothes were covered with mud by the time she arrived at the château.

Laughter reached her as she went inside and closed the door. Claudette was in the foyer. Nicole went to the stairs and sat down on the second step.

"Sounds as though my brother's celebration is still under way," she said, bracing herself as Claudette tugged the muddy boot off.

"Yes, Mademoiselle."

"He should be gone soon," Nicole assured her, "then things will be back to normal again."

Claudette took the boots and set them down carefully. "Will you be joining the others or do you want me to bring something up for you?"

"Neither. I'm not hungry. I'm going to bed. There's no need for you to have to cater to them all night. Give them another hour to wind down."

"Yes, Mademoiselle."

Nicole was exhausted and had started up the stairs when a peal of female laughter set her body to tingling. Camille was there! Nicole stopped and turned to Claudette who was busy with the boots at the bottom of the stairs.

"Are they still in the dining room?" she asked.

"Yes, Mademoiselle."

"When did Mademoiselle Cartier arrive?" Even saying Camille's name excited her.

"This morning."

"Where has she been all day? What has she been doing?"

"She and Antoine went riding earlier. I believe she even went on his first tour. He called her last evening and invited her here for a few days."

"I see." Nicole stood on the stairs, momentarily paralyzed until she heard Camille's voice filter through the other's. Unable to continue, Nicole descended the stairs and went directly to the dining room in her stocking feet.

The four of them were lingering over coffee, with Simon being the only one drinking wine. Antoine was reminiscing over a story from his childhood when he saw Nicole. Her cold, determined glare seemed to warm immediately the moment she saw Camille. The room was quiet as everyone waited for her to say something.

"Nickie," Lalo spoke up graciously. "I'm glad you could finally join us!"

She eyed the rest of the group sternly. Her stare eventually fell on Antoine. Nicole noticed how he squirmed in his chair. *As well he should,* she thought.

"I doubt seriously that I was even missed," Nicole said.

"Nonsense," Lalo bellowed, "we all noticed you

weren't here." He stood up clumsily and pulled a chair out for her. "Camille is a —"

"Antoine, may I speak to you for a moment?" Nicole said. Lalo's babbling only seemed to irritate her.

Antoine excused himself and followed her to the library.

"She's here as my guest," he said as soon as the library door was closed. "I assume it's permissible for me to have guests?"

"Yes, of course," Nicole said quietly. The fight was gone out of her. She was too tired to argue. "The servants will be available for another hour. I see no need to keep them at Lalo's disposal any longer than that." She turned slowly, sensing he was watching her. *He's brought her here for me,* she thought. *What a good friend he is.* "What do I say to her, Antoine? Tell me what to say."

His smile was reassuring as he nodded. "You'll know what to say. It's all in your heart."

Camille had watched Antoine and Nicole leave together and felt a total and unprecedented rejection like none she had ever experienced before. There was nothing left for her to do now but return to Paris first thing in the morning.

"How long have you known my sister?" Lalo asked, cutting into her thoughts.

"Only a few weeks," Camille said.

He smiled and leaned back in his chair as

Claudette brought in fresh coffee and tiny pastries. "Do you find Nicole attractive?"

Camille met his gaze boldly. "Yes. Very."

"I see." He then directed his smile to Simon who had a silly giggle that she hadn't noticed before.

"Do you have a problem with that?" she asked him.

"No, not at all," Lalo said waving his cup in the air. "Your perversions are your own business. I've often wondered what it is that two women could possibly see in each other. Nickie tried to explain it to me once."

"I'm sure I couldn't explain it any better," Camille said. "Lesbians have such imagination. We're the only ones to discover how wonderful sex without a penis can be. No mess. No waiting. Just one continuous orgasm after another!" She sighed dramatically. "As I said, it's the kind of thing we can't really explain. We're much too busy enjoying ourselves."

Lalo and Simon stared at her for a moment and then blinked dumbly several times before looking at one another. They shifted uneasily as Antoine came back in and returned to his seat. He poured himself a fresh cup of coffee before leaning closer to Camille.

"She's waiting for you in the library," he whispered.

Camille felt the familiar fluttering throughout her stomach. This was it. *Are we preparing for another argument? More tears? Will she demand that I return to Paris? Will I ever see her again after this?* Camille suddenly felt an acute aversion to the library.

Antoine nudged her with his elbow and whispered a sharp, "Go!" under his breath.

"Excuse me," she said meekly, moving away from the table. She found herself standing before the library door much too quickly and had the fear of hyperventilating before she could muster up the courage to go inside.

Chapter Fourteen

Nicole was gazing out the window when she heard the door softly open and then close again. Turning, she saw those sad brown eyes, so trusting yet unsure, and the tall, slender shape of Camille's body as she moved away from the door. *Everything about her is perfect,* Nicole thought. *I've loved her from the beginning. How could I have ever denied myself the pure pleasure of this woman's presence?*

Nicole knew she could not give her up, but she had no idea how to keep her. Antoine's words came back to her, his advice of speaking from her heart.

That would take care of things for now, but she wanted something for the future, something she could count on for a change. Her brother had severely damaged her trust in anyone.

There was so much Nicole wanted to say, so much she needed to say. Would she and Camille continue having only a weekend arrangement? Commuting from Dijon to Paris whenever they had a break in their schedules? Could they possibly ever live together? It hardly seemed feasible. The vineyards were in Nicole's blood, and Camille already had commitments of her own in Paris.

"Please sit down," Nicole said quietly. Camille moved to the sofa and sank into it. Nicole forced herself to stay near the corner of her desk several feet away. "First of all I want you to know that despite everything I've said in the past, I'm glad you're here. I've missed you terribly. I've said some dreadful things to you, and I want to apologize for every word that's brought you pain. It was never my intent to hurt you."

There was a sigh from the sofa as Nicole saw her close her eyes.

"I knew what I was doing at the time," Nicole continued, "and I had my reasons for doing it, but that didn't make it any easier for you and I'm very sorry." Her voice was low and brimming with emotion. Speaking from her heart was not as easy as Antoine had made it sound. "I first realized that I loved you when we were on our way to the villa. I felt as though you were the only thing in the world that mattered. Nothing could have stopped me from being with you. Nothing will ever stop me again. It's taken me a lifetime to find you, Camille, and I'm not about to lose you now." Their eyes met, and the love between them seemed to almost radiate across the room.

Camille sniffed and brushed away a tear that had rolled down her cheek. "You look so cute all caked in mud," she finally managed to say.

Nicole looked down at her riding clothes and her bootless feet and smiled. "I'm a mess."

"You're beautiful," Camille whispered. She rose from the sofa and went to her. Nicole trembled as Camille caressed her cheek lightly with her fingertips. "I can't help but touch you," she said, leaning closer to kiss her. They both trembled as their lips grazed each other. Camille pulled away slightly, but Nicole tightened her arms and then kissed her hungrily. Camille's soft lips brushed her throat, making her weak with desire.

"I've missed you so much," Nicole said breathlessly. "I've been crazy with worry."

"I was afraid you were going to send me away again."

"Never. I'll never send you away again." Nicole gently touched her cheek and hair. They kissed slowly, deeply, their tongues joining in an embrace of their own. "Come with me upstairs," Nicole whispered. They held hands the entire way.

They made love slowly, deliberately, each aware of nothing but the other. The curiosity and thrill of discovering a new lover was replaced by an overwhelming need to just be together in one another's arms again. Each kiss brought them closer than words ever could. They fell asleep together, their breathing synchronized and their bodies satisfied. Twilight in Burgundy cast an almost mystic spell over the château as they innocently slept. Morning was sure to arrive much too soon.

Camille woke before daybreak chilled to the bone. Nicole mumbled beside her and snuggled closer for warmth. Camille covered them up and cuddled into Nicole's soft body. She snapped awake when the door opened. Camille distinctly remembered seeing Nicole lock it from the inside before they had retired for the evening.

She lay petrified as the apparition moved slowly in the doorway. There was more of a faint glow of light rather than a distinct shape of any kind. Nicole softly mumbled again in her sleep.

Camille watched as the apparition hovered at the end of the bed. It was Eva. Camille sensed more than heard anything specific. The chill remained, but for some reason the whole ordeal seemed less threatening. As Eva's face became more visible, the wavering smile appeared more reassuring. Eva nodded slightly and then floated across the room before disappearing. Camille got up after a moment and closed and relocked the bedroom door. She slipped back into bed beside Nicole's warm, naked body and nuzzled into the soft curve of her back. Camille felt certain that the pounding of her heart could be heard all the way into the next room, but Nicole continued to sleep peacefully until daybreak.

The sun was in their eyes when they finally

woke. Camille gazed at Nicole who was propped on an elbow leaning over her with a smile much brighter and happier than the one she remembered from the evening before.

"Good morning," Camille said sleepily.

Nicole kissed her cheek. "Good morning," she said, rolling on top of her. Camille's hands moved easily down her back and pulled her even closer. They began to move against one another slowly as their bodies swam in a sea of pleasure. "Tell me what I have to do to convince you to come and live with me," Nicole murmured as Camille's lips nibbled her skin.

"Just ask me. That's all you've ever had to do."

Nicole's silence again left Camille with a feeling of uncertainty as to where she fit into her life. Even as Nicole kissed her throat eagerly she could feel the distance creeping back between them. There was still a barrier, something making it impossible for Nicole to give herself completely. Even the mere thought of making any type of commitment seemed to alienate her.

They made love slowly without the need for words, only soft utterances of pleasure. On a sexual level Camille was as sure of Nicole's feelings for her as she was of her own. There was no mistaking the tenderness of her touch and the passion in her eyes. They brought each other to heights neither had ever before experienced. Camille had been in love and involved in lengthy, wrenching relationships during her life, but Nicole Jeton added something different, something new and exciting. Her moodiness was a challenge, her temper a surprise.

Nicole's fingers carried her over the brink as she

held her tightly. A gentle kiss after a regular breathing pattern was restored gave Camille the need to hold her closer and run her hands through that wonderful hair. Nicole's blue eyes searched her face thoughtfully before she kissed her again.

"I love you," Nicole whispered huskily.

There, Camille thought. *She finally said it.* The wait was over, but for some reason doubts still remained.

"Do you?" Camille asked as she stroked her hair. "I believe you're afraid of me. Or at least afraid of anything permanent developing between us."

Nicole rolled over beside her and chuckled. "Where did you ever get such an idea?"

"The way you avoid certain aspects of our relationship. I had to practically trick you into admitting that you love me, and now I'll probably have to do the same thing to get you to say you want me to live with you. I've never known anyone who fought commitment so hard. I enjoy being pursued, Nicole. This would all be so much more pleasurable for me if some of it were your idea."

Nicole raised herself up on an elbow and slowly traced the dimples around Camille's mouth with a thin, delicate finger. "How can I explain this to you?" she whispered. "My whole way of life is about to change. Lalo is seeing to it that I'll be a pauper, and I'm not accustomed to poverty."

Camille listened to her, but couldn't comprehend what any of that had to do with their being together. She searched those blue eyes only inches from her own and resented being considered nothing more than an added burden to her problems.

"I don't understand what your financial situation

has to do with our life together," Camille said simply. "My baggage and I won't be arriving with the expectation of your having to support us. I'm more than capable of making a very good living here. I'm sure my qualifications would surprise you."

"Yes, indeed," Nicole said. "You've come highly recommended."

Camille eyed her furiously and threw the covers off. Within moments she was pulling on her clothes while Nicole lay back on the bed and stared at the ceiling.

"I knew you wouldn't understand."

"Understand what?" Camille snapped as she hurriedly buttoned her blouse. Her patience was surely being put to a test, she decided. Her anger, usually expressed in spiels of sarcasm at any given moment, was now composed of short-fused outbursts primed with energy. "That I'm in love with the most fickle woman I've ever met? That losing your precious inheritance is more important to you than I could ever be? One moment I'm convinced that you're crazy about me, and then in the next breath I'm not even sure you know I exist. Are you sure you love me, Nicole? Do you have any idea what the word means?"

"How can you say such things to me?" Nicole demanded as she scrambled out of bed and turned Camille around abruptly by the shoulders. "You've immobilized me. Opened my eyes to the possibility of a life I never thought I could have. Everything that happens now seems so important." She let her go and reached for her robe. "Then there's Lalo. He's draining me financially! Do you have any idea what that means? What it costs to keep the château in this condition? To keep it at least livable? To heat it in the winter? Not to mention the servants. I feel responsible for them, too. And the stables! The stables alone cost me a small fortune to maintain. It's possible I'll be with*out* all of that," she said. "You've given me a reason to want everything absolutely perfect here, Camille."

They stopped what they were doing, and each took a slow, steady breath. Their eyes searched one another.

"Why are we arguing?" Nicole finally asked. "And why are we putting on our clothes?"

Camille glanced down at her partially buttoned blouse as if amazed at how it had gotten on her body. Nicole took her by the hand and led her back to the bed.

"I'm not fickle," Nicole said as she began removing Camille's blouse again. "I'm in love with you. How could you ever doubt such a thing? My heart aches when you're away, Camille. I want you here with me. Living here. Sleeping here. Eating here. I don't know how else to say it."

"You're certainly doing much better," Camille purred into her neck.

"I can't believe I met you during the worst time of my life," Nicole said. Camille pulled the robe off of her shoulders and then gently urged Nicole back on the bed. "With Papa gone and then Lalo showing up again. Lalo makes me crazy." Camille's mouth was on her throat and at the soft curve of her neck. Nicole found it difficult to think or talk. "I'm not fickle," she whispered breathlessly. "Really. I'm not." Camille's mouth moved down her stomach, and caused a wonderful throbbing between Nicole's legs. "God, how I want you," Nicole breathed as Camille buried her tongue in the center of her very existence. They were both exhausted by the time they fell asleep again.

Chapter Fifteen

Camille napped again after a bubble bath with Nicole. When she woke she felt refreshed and hungry, and she was looking forward to the quiet peacefulness that the château offered during the day. Nicole had left earlier for an appointment with her lawyer and wasn't expected back for several hours. They had agreed to talk about their future living arrangements later that afternoon.

Camille selected her clothes, dressed slowly, and wallowed in the luxury of not having anything to do. Her visits to Dijon were making her more aware of the simple, hard-working way of life that the people in Burgundy had, as opposed to the hustle and often congested nature of the city. Camille had never lived in the country, but she was certain that she could adapt to it quite nicely.

Her career, however, was something she needed to think about. Camille was doing well with the magazine and expected to be promoted again within a year, but she had no qualms about leaving and seeking employment elsewhere. She didn't have time to do any serious writing of her own any longer. The life of a junior editor was an all-consuming position, often leaving her mentally drained. She liked the exhaustion and the money, even though the job itself at times was unfulfilling. The challenge, however, was nothing compared to the rigors she had encountered in her early days as a teacher.

Camille had spent the first four years out of college teaching journalism in a private school. During that time she had numerous articles published and a convincing bite on a column that was then only in the planning stages. In addition to her promising career, she had found the time to fall in love and set up housekeeping with a beautiful dancer she had met during an interview.

They had been happy for over two years until her lover began touring with a dance troupe. Before long telephone calls stopped and letters failed to arrive. Things were never the same between them when her lover finally returned, and they spent their last few months together going through the various stages of breaking up.

They still saw each other occasionally and had many of the same friends. Only in the last few years had they really been able to enjoy each other's company again. If they had worked as hard on their relationship as they had on their friendship, no doubt they would still be together.

Leaving her Parisian life behind for a more tranquil and meaningful existence somewhere else didn't seem to be much of a sacrifice. Camille would be able to resume writing again or possibly even teach in a local school at some point in the future. Nicole had finally been able to convince her that she wanted them to be together. Just the thought of being able to see Nicole every day made Camille squirm a little as she sat on the edge of the bed to put on her shoes. *How much work will either of us get done if we live together?* she wondered with a chuckle. No one would see them for at least the first two months.

Camille went downstairs and found Claudette closing the front door. No matter what time of day it was, the young maid appeared impeccably starched. Her rosy cheeks and blond hair probably disguised her age well, Camille decided.

"Good morning, Mademoiselle," Claudette said pleasantly. "Breakfast?"

"Something light, please." Camille went to the dining room and glanced at her watch. It was ten-thirty, and she was embarrassed by the lateness of the morning. "The servants probably think you're as lazy as Lalo," she muttered to herself as Claudette came in with sliced fruit and cheese. "Is Antoine at the winery?" Camille asked.

"He's in the library with the Marquis," Claudette said shyly.

As Camille peeled an orange and sipped her tea, she heard angry male voices coming from the end of the hall. She tried to ignore what they were saying, having no desire to eavesdrop on anyone, but their voices carried in such a way that she had no choice but to listen. Apparently they hadn't closed the library door.

Lalo paced back and forth in his Marquis suit, one of the three replicas of his grandfather's outfit that had been specially tailored for him. Antoine leaned against the desk and rubbed his chin nervously.

"You like your job here, Antoine?" Lalo asked.

"Of course."

"How much do you like it?" Lalo continued pacing back and forth with his hands behind his back. "It's time that my sister learned a few things about you."

"Meaning?"

"The beginning, Antoine. Remember how you helped me spend all that money? How you helped me get more every time Nickie refused to give me a loan? You were more than willing to empty her bank account month after month. You remember that, don't you?"

"I made a mistake, Lalo!" Antoine stammered. "A terrible mistake. I was stupid to side with you. Even for a moment."

"But you did," Lalo reminded him pointedly. "Some of it might even have been your idea."

"That was another lifetime, Lalo."

"All the same . . ."

"So you've called this little meeting to try to blackmail me? Is that it?"

Lalo smiled. "I could be persuaded to keep our secret for a price, my friend."

"I don't have any money."

Lalo threw his head back and laughed. "You drive a new car. Wear nice clothes. Are you trying to make me believe that my sister supports you?" When Antoine didn't answer, Lalo laughed again. "For twenty thousand I can keep a secret."

"Nicole won't listen to you."

"Are you willing to take that chance?" Lalo countered. "I can give her specifics. Meeting places. Conversations. My memory's quite good on this." Lalo smiled wickedly. "But for twenty thousand I could forget a few things."

Antoine closed his eyes and shook his head wearily. "I can't pay you that kind of money."

"Then Nicole will know everything there is to know about you," he said simply. His laughter echoed down the hallway making everyone who heard it uneasy.

Camille resumed eating her breakfast and listened as Lalo snapped orders to the maid from the foyer. Camille felt as though she had to let Nicole know about what she had overheard, but she wasn't sure how much of this was any of her business. A few minutes later Antoine came into the dining room and slumped into his chair.

"He's crazy," he said after a moment. "He can destroy us all if he wants to."

Camille eyed him steadily. "How much of what he said is true?" Antoine's despair had little effect on her as she spoke.

"How much of what?"

"I overheard you and Lalo talking," she said. "Did you ever try to help him get Nicole's money?"

Antoine raked his fingers through his dark wavy hair and got up from the table. He tried to leave, but Camille was right behind him every step of the way. She finally grabbed his arm as he reached the front door.

"Tell me everything, and I mean everything," Camille seethed. "I'm not sure how much more Nicole can take, but I promise you one thing, Antoine. Any deceit from you will hurt her much more than anything Lalo could ever do. She expects it from him. She doesn't expect it from you."

"I was stupid, Camille," he said, eyes wide with despair. "I loved him so much then. He could talk me into anything!" He was almost in tears as he looked at her. "Help me," he whispered.

Camille yanked him into the drawing room and closed the door. She led him to the sofa and gave him a few moments to pull himself together.

"Tell me everything about you, Lalo, and the money," she said calmly. Yelling at him wouldn't make him talk any faster, she decided.

Antoine sniffed a few times and avoided looking at her. He ran his fingers through his hair again. "After their father became ill, Nicole left school and came to help us with the winery. Lalo was glad to

151

hand everything over to her. She was so good at it. Lalo began drinking a lot more almost immediately and then started gambling. He stayed out late and was sometimes gone for days at a time. I'm sure now that he was seeing other men, but at the time he convinced me that it was his drinking that kept him away. He told me about waking up in strange places sometimes and not knowing how he got there. I believed him, of course," he said heavily. "I always believed him."

"Was he borrowing money from Nicole then?"

"I don't think so. He had a generous amount of his own, but he went through it very quickly."

"Lalo mentioned your helping empty Nicole's bank account," Camille said. "Tell me what happened."

Antoine got up and walked to the window. He turned around but avoided looking at her. "Lalo and I had been drinking together one evening, and I suggested that he ask her for a loan. We were going to leave together after that. I ended up meeting him somewhere a few days later." Antoine came back to the sofa and sat down again. "I loved him so much. I probably would have done anything for him. I have no other excuse. We met in Morocco, but I only stayed with him two days. I hated his friends. The fast cars. Gambling and drinking all night long. He was just *throw*ing money away. I couldn't watch him do it any more. I came back to Dijon and began taking my work seriously." Antoine stopped and looked at Camille, but she kept her expression unreadable. He moved to the end of the sofa next to her chair and took her hand in his.

"In the beginning neither of us were much good to Nicole. She got the winery back in shape with

152

very little help from me or Lalo. She and I didn't really know each other well in those days. I was just someone Lalo brought home one night. I stayed in the cellar doing what I was trained to do, and Nicole stayed in the lab. My talents as a cellarmaster never really registered with her at first, mainly because I was too busy worrying about Lalo and following him around."

Antoine looked at her with eager, liquid eyes. "There's another part of this story that I think you should know about. It's much more important than what I've just told you. It's the part where I finally began to know Nicole. Once Lalo was gone, she and I spent more time together. She was so generous and trusting. She opened her home to me, offered friendship, and understanding. Those first few months after Lalo left I felt so guilty staying here and accepting all she wanted to give me, until I realized that Nicole needed me as much as I needed her. A job, a home, a friend! That side of her I would've never gotten to know if Lalo had stayed. His leaving was the best thing that ever happened to me!"

Camille, reassured by his sincerity, gave his warm hand a friendly pat. "The best thing for you to do is tell Nicole everything. Lalo won't be able to hurt you then."

The front door slammed and loud angry voices boomed from the foyer. It was Nicole and Lalo yelling at each other as if they were acres apart instead of in the same room.

"I don't believe you!" Nicole shouted on her way

to the library. "Antoine is no longer under your spell. He came to his senses years ago!"

"You think so?" Lalo roared as he slammed a door, shutting off Camille and Antoine's access to their conversation. "You don't think he would come with me if I asked him to?"

"No," she said. "He's finished with you."

"Don't be so sure." Lalo adjusted the red scarf around his neck. "You would keep him here knowing what he tried to do to you?" They had at least stopped yelling at one another. "There are so many ways, Nickie. So many ways. What if word gets out that you're a lesbian? How much wine could you sell *then*?"

Nicole glared at him. "My wine is good enough to overcome any obstacle you put in my way. When you're one of the best, Lalo, people tend to forget whom you sleep with." She was, of course, bluffing. Nicole had no idea what would happen to her business if the wine industry discovered that she was a lesbian, but she had no intention of letting him know any of that. "How dare you threaten me with such a thing," she snapped. "You of all people should know better."

He tugged on his scarf again and tossed his hair away from his forehead. "Do you have my money?"

Nicole glared at him once more. "I can't liquidate some of my assets for at least another week. I'll need more time."

He drew himself up to his full six foot two height. "I can't wait that long." His voice was calm as he folded his arms across his chest. "How much do you have available now?" he asked after a moment.

"A little over half, but I have a few more stipulations of my own before I'll agree to give you the rest of it."

"Ha!" he said as he threw his head back. "What kind of stipulations? You've already talked me out of claiming my half of the château."

Nicole opened her briefcase and took out a document. "I retain the full use of the Jeton name when it comes to wine or winemaking. You can't use it in any way for business purposes."

"My *name*?" he bellowed. "You're asking me to sell you my *name*?"

"Your investments never work, Lalo. As soon as you throw this money away, you'll be back for more. In the meantime I can't have you jetting all over the world pretending that the Jeton winery has branched out somewhere else. You'll ruin me."

"You can't stop me from using the Jeton name. It's *my* name," he said, thumping his chest.

"Sign this paper and I'll give you the rest of the money."

Lalo turned around. Nicole stepped back away from him and felt a sudden chill in the room. Eva was there, but Lalo apparently hadn't noticed. He was too busy flexing what little muscle he had.

"You're trying to cheat me," he said as he stood in front of her and put his hands on her shoulders. "I don't like that. You're trying to cheat me."

Nicole felt every fiber in her body become tense as Lalo's fingers slowly moved along her shoulders. His left hand slid behind her neck in a rough, icy grasp.

"My name isn't for sale."

"Let go of me."

155

"My home. My life. My self-respect," Lalo said in a strangely calm voice. "Eva did the same thing to Philippe, didn't she? Everything had to be her way. She made him do it, Nickie. Eva drove him to it. She made him kill her." With a jerk he pulled Nicole even closer to him and covered her throat with his other hand. "This was the only way he could get what he wanted from her, wasn't it?"

His eyes were bulging, glassy marbles, and Nicole could see the hatred he had for her. "Lalo," she whispered only moments before he tightened his grip and the room began to spin.

Chapter Sixteen

Camille rested her head on the back of the chair and kept her eyes on Eva's portrait. She would never get tired of looking at it. *What a beautiful woman,* she mused. *And never married!*

"Have they always yelled at each other like this?" Camille asked.

Antoine nodded. "Oh, yes. Nicole has very little patience as it is, but where Lalo's concerned she has none."

"Obviously." Camille continued looking at the portrait. Eva's eyes were as blue as Nicole's, and both women had a presence about them that commanded respect even at a glance.

"I believe my time here at the château is coming to an end," Antoine said. He stood up and finished the wine in his glass. "I'm going down there."

"This is between them, Antoine."

"If your future rested in Lalo's hands, would *you* sit here?"

They both turned as the door behind them opened and Simon the twit came in. Camille found it a relief to see doors that finally opened for a reason.

"Excuse me. I thought Lalo might be in here." Simon's cologne reached them both before he was in the room all the way.

"No, I'm sorry," Camille said. "He's with Nicole in the library." Moments later they heard the roar of the wind and could feel the floor under their feet begin to shake. The château seemed to be rumbling all around them. They looked at one another and in unison started down the long hallway toward the library.

The cold air gave Nicole the strength to stay conscious as Lalo began crushing her vocal cords, but Eva was there waiting for him on her behalf.

Eva's untimely death at the hands of her own brother so many years earlier had kept her aware of an unfulfilled need. As records and diaries would indicate, Eva's restlessness at the château had begun the day Nicole was born.

The wind, virtually coming from nowhere, started to blow inside the room. The roar threatened to deafen them. Nicole grabbed Lalo's hands and tried to pull them away from her throat, but she was no match for a madman. His glassy eyes and parted lips were only inches from her own as he gripped even tighter. They struggled against the powerful arctic gusts that seemed to be getting stronger. Nicole was not ready to die this way; she pounded at him frantically with her fists.

Lalo suddenly began shaking in short spastic movements. He released her and grabbed his head, screaming pathetically as his body slammed into the bookcase across the room. He fell to the floor in a heap with the wind continuing to batter them both.

Hearing the commotion inside, Camille, Antoine, and Simon tried to force the library door open, but it would only move an inch or so at the most with all three of their mutual efforts combined. They pushed and shoved while the clamor continued from within, but the door wouldn't open.

"Push harder!" Camille shouted over the howling coming from the other side.

Almost as suddenly as it began, the wind seemed to stop, causing the three in the hallway to tumble into the room. Camille scrambled to her feet and saw Nicole leaning against the desk coughing and clutching her throat. The room was quiet and calm, appearing exactly as it had only minutes before. Nicole's labored breathing spurred them all into action.

Camille took her in her arms and felt Nicole shiver. She pulled her closer into the warmth of her body.

"What happened, darling?" Camille asked as she hugged her.

"Lalo . . ." was all Nicole could say before she started to cough again. Her voice was almost gone. Camille held her tightly and continued to rub Nicole's body to get the blood circulating again.

"Sit down over here," Camille said as she helped her to the sofa. "Antoine, get her some water." Camille eyed Lalo on the floor. He didn't look like a threat to anyone any longer. Simon hurried to help him, while Camille turned her attention back to her lover.

Antoine brought the water over and tried to help her with it, but Nicole had trouble swallowing and started to cough again. She dropped her head on Camille's shoulder and eventually stopped shaking.

"Is he dead?" she managed to ask in a hoarse whisper.

"No." Camille had seen Lalo open his eyes briefly earlier.

"I want him out of here," Nicole said. "Tell him," she rasped between quick breaths and random coughs, "tell him that next time Eva will kill him." She sank even farther into Camille's arms and watched Simon drag her brother out of the library.

Camille held her for several minutes, kissing the top of Nicole's head as they huddled together. Nicole had grown so still that Camille was beginning to wonder if she had fallen asleep.

"He tried to kill me," Nicole finally said in a strained, weak voice.

Camille kissed her cheek and had her own tears to deal with. "Eva took care of him. She's been waiting for this for a long time. Try not to think about it. Lalo's gone now."

Nicole raised her head and pushed a lock of hair

out of her eyes before seeing Antoine clearly on the other side of the room. She managed to stand up on trembling, unsteady legs and tried to drink from her water glass. She rubbed her throat gingerly.

"I'm very tired," she said as the normalness of her voice began to return. "He tried to kill me."

Camille watched her closely and saw the red marks on her throat that would surely be bruises by morning. There was a distant look in those wonderful blue eyes that filled Camille with a sadness like none she had ever known. *She's so vulnerable.* Camille wanted to take her in her arms again and make it all better, but she felt certain that Nicole didn't need that from her now.

"Antoine," Nicole said in a quiet, strained voice.

He looked at her from across the room like a scolded child. "Yes, Nicole."

"Have him sign this paper and then get an address where I can send him his money. If he refuses to sign," she continued hoarsely, "then he gets nothing from me. Do you understand?"

"Yes." Antoine took the paper from her.

"And tell him," Nicole said as her voice lapsed in and out of a whisper, "tell him that if he ever comes back, I'll have him arrested. I'm filing a report in the morning. And remind him, Antoine, that Eva will gladly kill him the next time."

Antoine nodded and left the room. Camille was relieved when he finally closed the door. She held her hand out and Nicole returned to the sofa. They touched easily, brushing away mutual tears. Camille traced a welt that had formed on the side of Nicole's neck as her own hatred for Lalo Jeton slowly began to churn.

"He tried to kill me," Nicole said as she once again rubbed her throat. There was a sense of wonder in her voice, as if everything that had just happened to her still didn't seem real.

"Lalo's gone now," Camille said. "He won't be back."

The temperature in the room began to drop and made them both sink even farther into each other. Nicole laid her head on Camille's shoulder again and settled into the comfort of her arms. "Eva likes you," she whispered. "I've learned to trust her judgment in women."

"She's made a wise choice this time," Camille offered as she caught the sweet scent of Nicole's hair. They sat there together not saying anything for a long time. Nicole reached over and took Camille's hand.

"Do you still want to stay with me after all of this?"

"Of course I do," Camille said. There was a little flutter in her stomach as Nicole slowly unbuttoned the top two buttons on Camille's blouse and nuzzled into the safe haven of her bare shoulder. The need just to be close seemed to be almost overwhelming. Nicole kissed her several times at the soft hollow of her throat.

"This thing Eva does with the wind," Camille said after a moment. "The howling and the flying bodies and such. Exactly how often does she do this sort of thing?"

"Not often."

"How often?" Camille pressed with a hint of a smile. She was amused by her own need for specifics. "Suppose you and I are having a little disagreement

162

some afternoon, or a few heated words at some point like most lovers eventually do." There was more fumbling with another button on her blouse. "Will I find myself in the middle of a blizzard in the foyer some day? Does she do this sort of thing often?"

Nicole leaned over and kissed her very lightly on the lips. "Not often."

Camille cocked her head to get a better look at her. "How often?"

"If you have your hands on my throat at the time that we're yelling at each other, then you might have a problem, but other than that I wouldn't worry about it. We've had some very nice arguments here already," Nicole reminded her.

"But I prefer arguing without all that wind," Camille said. "Just regular, uneventful, generic arguing. Could you talk to Eva about that?"

Nicole smiled and resumed working on the rest of the buttons. "We'll see."

A few of the publications of
THE NAIAD PRESS, INC.
P.O. Box 10543 • Tallahassee, Florida 32302
Phone (904) 539-5965
Toll-Free Order Number: 1-800-533-1973
Mail orders welcome. Please include 15% postage.

NORTHERN BLUE by Tracey Richardson. 224 pp. Police recruits
Miki & Miranda — passion in the line of fire. ISBN 1-56280-118-X $10.95

LOVE'S HARVEST by Peggy Herring. 176 pp. by the author of
Once More With Feeling.   ISBN 1-56280-117-1   10.95

THE COLOR OF WINTER by Lisa Shapiro. 208 pp. Romantic
love beyond your wildest dreams.   ISBN 1-56280-116-3   10.95

FAMILY SECRETS by Laura DeHart Young. 208 pp. Enthralling
romance and suspense.   ISBN 1-56280-119-8   10.95

INLAND PASSAGE by Jane Rule. 288 pp. Tales exploring conven-
tional & unconventional relationships.   ISBN 0-930044-56-8   10.95

DOUBLE BLUFF by Claire McNab. 208 pp. 7th Detective Carol
Ashton Mystery.   ISBN 1-56280-096-5   10.95

BAR GIRLS by Lauran Hoffman. 176 pp. See the movie, read
the book!   ISBN 1-56280-115-5   10.95

THE FIRST TIME EVER edited by Barbara Grier & Christine
Cassidy. 272 pp. Love stories by Naiad Press authors.
     ISBN 1-56280-086-8   14.95

MISS PETTIBONE AND MISS McGRAW by Brenda Weathers.
208 pp. A charming ghostly love story.   ISBN 1-56280-151-1   10.95

CHANGES by Jackie Calhoun. 208 pp. Involved romance and
relationships.   ISBN 1-56280-083-3   10.95

FAIR PLAY by Rose Beecham. 256 pp. 3rd Amanda Valentine
Mystery.   ISBN 1-56280-081-7   10.95

PAXTON COURT by Diane Salvatore. 256 pp. Erotic and wickedly
funny contemporary tale about the business of learning to live
together.   ISBN 1-56280-109-0   21.95

PAYBACK by Celia Cohen. 176 pp. A gripping thriller of romance,
revenge and betrayal.   ISBN 1-56280-084-1   10.95

THE BEACH AFFAIR by Barbara Johnson. 224 pp. Sizzling
summer romance/mystery/intrigue.   ISBN 1-56280-090-6   10.95

GETTING THERE by Robbi Sommers. 192 pp. Nobody does it
like Robbi!   ISBN 1-56280-099-X   10.95

FINAL CUT by Lisa Haddock. 208 pp. 2nd Carmen Ramirez
Mystery.   ISBN 1-56280-088-4   10.95

FLASHPOINT by Katherine V. Forrest. 256 pp. A Lesbian
blockbuster!   ISBN 1-56280-079-5   10.95

CLAIRE OF THE MOON by Nicole Conn. Audio Book —Read
by Marianne Hyatt.   ISBN 1-56280-113-9   16.95

FOR LOVE AND FOR LIFE: INTIMATE PORTRAITS OF
LESBIAN COUPLES by Susan Johnson. 224 pp.
                                                ISBN 1-56280-091-4   14.95

DEVOTION by Mindy Kaplan. 192 pp. See the movie — read
the book!   ISBN 1-56280-093-0   10.95

SOMEONE TO WATCH by Jaye Maiman. 272 pp. 4th Robin
Miller Mystery.   ISBN 1-56280-095-7   10.95

GREENER THAN GRASS by Jennifer Fulton. 208 pp. A young
woman — a stranger in her bed.   ISBN 1-56280-092-2   10.95

TRAVELS WITH DIANA HUNTER by Regine Sands. Erotic
lesbian romp. Audio Book (2 cassettes)   ISBN 1-56280-107-4   16.95

CABIN FEVER by Carol Schmidt. 256 pp. Sizzling suspense
and passion.   ISBN 1-56280-089-1   10.95

THERE WILL BE NO GOODBYES by Laura DeHart Young. 192
pp. Romantic love, strength, and friendship.   ISBN 1-56280-103-1   10.95

FAULTLINE by Sheila Ortiz Taylor. 144 pp. Joyous comic
lesbian novel.   ISBN 1-56280-108-2   9.95

OPEN HOUSE by Pat Welch. 176 pp. 4th Helen Black Mystery.
                                                ISBN 1-56280-102-3   10.95

ONCE MORE WITH FEELING by Peggy J. Herring. 240 pp.
Lighthearted, loving romantic adventure.   ISBN 1-56280-089-2   10.95

FOREVER by Evelyn Kennedy. 224 pp. Passionate romance — love
overcoming all obstacles.   ISBN 1-56280-094-9   10.95

WHISPERS by Kris Bruyer. 176 pp. Romantic ghost story
                                                ISBN 1-56280-082-5   10.95

NIGHT SONGS by Penny Mickelbury. 224 pp. 2nd Gianna Maglione
Mystery.   ISBN 1-56280-097-3   10.95

GETTING TO THE POINT by Teresa Stores. 256 pp. Classic
southern Lesbian novel.   ISBN 1-56280-100-7   10.95

PAINTED MOON by Karin Kallmaker. 224 pp. Delicious
Kallmaker romance.   ISBN 1-56280-075-2   10.95

THE MYSTERIOUS NAIAD edited by Katherine V. Forrest &
Barbara Grier. 320 pp. Love stories by Naiad Press authors.
                                                ISBN 1-56280-074-4   14.95

DAUGHTERS OF A CORAL DAWN by Katherine V. Forrest.
240 pp. Tenth Anniversay Edition.   ISBN 1-56280-104-X   10.95

BODY GUARD by Claire McNab. 208 pp. 6th Carol Ashton
Mystery.   ISBN 1-56280-073-6   10.95

CACTUS LOVE by Lee Lynch. 192 pp. Stories by the beloved
storyteller.   ISBN 1-56280-071-X   9.95

SECOND GUESS by Rose Beecham. 216 pp. 2nd Amanda Valentine
Mystery.   ISBN 1-56280-069-8   9.95

THE SURE THING by Melissa Hartman. 208 pp. L.A. earthquake
romance.   ISBN 1-56280-078-7   9.95

A RAGE OF MAIDENS by Lauren Wright Douglas. 240 pp. 6th Caitlin
Reece Mystery.   ISBN 1-56280-068-X   10.95

TRIPLE EXPOSURE by Jackie Calhoun. 224 pp. Romantic drama
involving many characters.   ISBN 1-56280-067-1   9.95

UP, UP AND AWAY by Catherine Ennis. 192 pp. Delightful
romance.   ISBN 1-56280-065-5   9.95

PERSONAL ADS by Robbi Sommers. 176 pp. Sizzling short
stories.   ISBN 1-56280-059-0   9.95

FLASHPOINT by Katherine V. Forrest. 256 pp. Lesbian
blockbuster!   ISBN 1-56280-043-4   22.95

CROSSWORDS by Penny Sumner. 256 pp. 2nd Victoria Cross
Mystery.   ISBN 1-56280-064-7   9.95

SWEET CHERRY WINE by Carol Schmidt. 224 pp. A novel of
suspense.   ISBN 1-56280-063-9   9.95

CERTAIN SMILES by Dorothy Tell. 160 pp. Erotic short stories.
                                           ISBN 1-56280-066-3   9.95

EDITED OUT by Lisa Haddock. 224 pp. 1st Carmen Ramirez
Mystery.   ISBN 1-56280-077-9   9.95

WEDNESDAY NIGHTS by Camarin Grae. 288 pp. Sexy
adventure.   ISBN 1-56280-060-4   10.95

SMOKEY O by Celia Cohen. 176 pp. Relationships on the
playing field.   ISBN 1-56280-057-4   9.95

KATHLEEN O'DONALD by Penny Hayes. 256 pp. Rose and
Kathleen find each other and employment in 1909 NYC.
                                           ISBN 1-56280-070-1   9.95

STAYING HOME by Elisabeth Nonas. 256 pp. Molly and Alix
want a baby . . . or do they?   ISBN 1-56280-076-0   10.95

TRUE LOVE by Jennifer Fulton. 240 pp. Six lesbians searching
for love in all the "right" places.   ISBN 1-56280-035-3   10.95

GARDENIAS WHERE THERE ARE NONE by Molleen Zanger.
176 pp. Why is Melanie inextricably drawn to the old house?
                                           ISBN 1-56280-056-6   9.95

KEEPING SECRETS by Penny Mickelbury. 208 pp. 1st Gianna
Maglione Mystery.   ISBN 1-56280-052-3   9.95

THE ROMANTIC NAIAD edited by Katherine V. Forrest &
Barbara Grier. 336 pp. Love stories by Naiad Press authors.
ISBN 1-56280-054-X   14.95

UNDER MY SKIN by Jaye Maiman. 336 pp. 3rd Robin Miller
Mystery.   ISBN 1-56280-049-3.   10.95

STAY TOONED by Rhonda Dicksion. 144 pp. Cartoons — 1st
collection since *Lesbian Survival Manual.*   ISBN 1-56280-045-0   9.95

CAR POOL by Karin Kallmaker. 272pp. Lesbians on wheels
and then some!   ISBN 1-56280-048-5   10.95

NOT TELLING MOTHER: STORIES FROM A LIFE by Diane
Salvatore. 176 pp. Her 3rd novel.   ISBN 1-56280-044-2   9.95

GOBLIN MARKET by Lauren Wright Douglas. 240pp. 5th Caitlin
Reece Mystery.   ISBN 1-56280-047-7   10.95

LONG GOODBYES by Nikki Baker. 256 pp. 3rd Virginia Kelly
Mystery.   ISBN 1-56280-042-6   9.95

FRIENDS AND LOVERS by Jackie Calhoun. 224 pp. Mid-
western Lesbian lives and loves.   ISBN 1-56280-041-8   10.95

THE CAT CAME BACK by Hilary Mullins. 208 pp. Highly
praised Lesbian novel.   ISBN 1-56280-040-X   9.95

BEHIND CLOSED DOORS by Robbi Sommers. 192 pp. Hot,
erotic short stories.   ISBN 1-56280-039-6   9.95

CLAIRE OF THE MOON by Nicole Conn. 192 pp. See the
movie — read the book!   ISBN 1-56280-038-8   10.95

SILENT HEART by Claire McNab. 192 pp. Exotic Lesbian
romance.   ISBN 1-56280-036-1   10.95

HAPPY ENDINGS by Kate Brandt. 272 pp. Intimate conversations
with Lesbian authors.   ISBN 1-56280-050-7   10.95

THE SPY IN QUESTION by Amanda Kyle Williams. 256 pp.
4th Madison McGuire Mystery.   ISBN 1-56280-037-X   9.95

SAVING GRACE by Jennifer Fulton. 240 pp. Adventure and
romantic entanglement.   ISBN 1-56280-051-5   9.95

THE YEAR SEVEN by Molleen Zanger. 208 pp. Women surviving
in a new world.   ISBN 1-56280-034-5   9.95

CURIOUS WINE by Katherine V. Forrest. 176 pp. Tenth Anniver-
sary Edition. The most popular contemporary Lesbian love story.
ISBN 1-56280-053-1   10.95
     Audio Book (2 cassettes)   ISBN 1-56280-105-8   16.95

CHAUTAUQUA by Catherine Ennis. 192 pp. Exciting, romantic
adventure.   ISBN 1-56280-032-9   9.95

A PROPER BURIAL by Pat Welch. 192 pp. 3rd Helen Black
Mystery.   ISBN 1-56280-033-7   9.95

SILVERLAKE HEAT: A Novel of Suspense by Carol Schmidt.
240 pp. Rhonda is as hot as Laney's dreams.   ISBN 1-56280-031-0   9.95

LOVE, ZENA BETH by Diane Salvatore. 224 pp. The most talked
about lesbian novel of the nineties!   ISBN 1-56280-030-2   10.95

A DOORYARD FULL OF FLOWERS by Isabel Miller. 160 pp.
Stories incl. 2 sequels to *Patience and Sarah.*   ISBN 1-56280-029-9   9.95

MURDER BY TRADITION by Katherine V. Forrest. 288 pp. 4th
Kate Delafield Mystery.   ISBN 1-56280-002-7   10.95

THE EROTIC NAIAD edited by Katherine V. Forrest & Barbara
Grier. 224 pp. Love stories by Naiad Press authors.
ISBN 1-56280-026-4   14.95

DEAD CERTAIN by Claire McNab. 224 pp. 5th Carol Ashton
Mystery.   ISBN 1-56280-027-2   9.95

CRAZY FOR LOVING by Jaye Maiman. 320 pp. 2nd Robin Miller
Mystery.   ISBN 1-56280-025-6   9.95

STONEHURST by Barbara Johnson. 176 pp. Passionate regency
romance.   ISBN 1-56280-024-8   10.95

INTRODUCING AMANDA VALENTINE by Rose Beecham.
256 pp. 1st Amanda Valentine Mystery.   ISBN 1-56280-021-3   9.95

UNCERTAIN COMPANIONS by Robbi Sommers. 204 pp.
Steamy, erotic novel.   ISBN 1-56280-017-5   9.95

A TIGER'S HEART by Lauren W. Douglas. 240 pp. 4th.Caitlin
Reece Mystery.   ISBN 1-56280-018-3   9.95

PAPERBACK ROMANCE by Karin Kallmaker. 256 pp. A
delicious romance.   ISBN 1-56280-019-1   9.95

MORTON RIVER VALLEY by Lee Lynch. 304 pp. Lee Lynch
at her best!   ISBN 1-56280-016-7   9.95

THE LAVENDER HOUSE MURDER by Nikki Baker. 224 pp.
2nd Virginia Kelly Mystery.   ISBN 1-56280-012-4   9.95

PASSION BAY by Jennifer Fulton. 224 pp. Passionate romance,
virgin beaches, tropical skies.   ISBN 1-56280-028-0   10.95

STICKS AND STONES by Jackie Calhoun. 208 pp. Contemporary
lesbian lives and loves.   ISBN 1-56280-020-5   9.95
Audio Book (2 cassettes)   ISBN 1-56280-106-6   16.95

DELIA IRONFOOT by Jeane Harris. 192 pp. Adventure for Delia
and Beth in the Utah mountains.   ISBN 1-56280-014-0   9.95

UNDER THE SOUTHERN CROSS by Claire McNab. 192 pp.
Romantic nights Down Under.   ISBN 1-56280-011-6   9.95

GRASSY FLATS by Penny Hayes. 256 pp. Lesbian romance in
the '30s.   ISBN 1-56280-010-8   9.95

A SINGULAR SPY by Amanda K. Williams. 192 pp. 3rd
Madison McGuire Mystery.   ISBN 1-56280-008-6   8.95

THE END OF APRIL by Penny Sumner. 240 pp. 1st Victoria
Cross Mystery.   ISBN 1-56280-007-8   8.95

HOUSTON TOWN by Deborah Powell. 208 pp. A Hollis
Carpenter Mystery.   ISBN 1-56280-006-X   8.95

KISS AND TELL by Robbi Sommers. 192 pp. Scorching stories
by the author of *Pleasures*.   ISBN 1-56280-005-1   10.95

STILL WATERS by Pat Welch. 208 pp. 2nd Helen Black Mystery.
                                        ISBN 0-941483-97-5   9.95

TO LOVE AGAIN by Evelyn Kennedy. 208 pp. Wildly romantic
love story.   ISBN 0-941483-85-1   9.95

IN THE GAME by Nikki Baker. 192 pp. 1st Virginia Kelly
Mystery.   ISBN 1-56280-004-3   9.95

AVALON by Mary Jane Jones. 256 pp. A Lesbian Arthurian
romance.   ISBN 0-941483-96-7   9.95

STRANDED by Camarin Grae. 320 pp. Entertaining, riveting
adventure.   ISBN 0-941483-99-1   9.95

THE DAUGHTERS OF ARTEMIS by Lauren Wright Douglas.
240 pp. 3rd Caitlin Reece Mystery.   ISBN 0-941483-95-9   9.95

CLEARWATER by Catherine Ennis. 176 pp. Romantic secrets
of a small Louisiana town.   ISBN 0-941483-65-7   8.95

THE HALLELUJAH MURDERS by Dorothy Tell. 176 pp. 2nd
Poppy Dillworth Mystery.   ISBN 0-941483-88-6   8.95

SECOND CHANCE by Jackie Calhoun. 256 pp. Contemporary
Lesbian lives and loves.   ISBN 0-941483-93-2   9.95

BENEDICTION by Diane Salvatore. 272 pp. Striking, contemporary romantic novel.   ISBN 0-941483-90-8   9.95

BLACK IRIS by Jeane Harris. 192 pp. Caroline's hidden past . . .
                                        ISBN 0-941483-68-1   8.95

TOUCHWOOD by Karin Kallmaker. 240 pp. Loving, May/
December romance.   ISBN 0-941483-76-2   9.95

COP OUT by Claire McNab. 208 pp. 4th Carol Ashton Mystery.
                                        ISBN 0-941483-84-3   9.95

THE BEVERLY MALIBU by Katherine V. Forrest. 288 pp. 3rd
Kate Delafield Mystery.   ISBN 0-941483-48-7   10.95

THAT OLD STUDEBAKER by Lee Lynch. 272 pp. Andy's affair
with Regina and her attachment to her beloved car.
                                        ISBN 0-941483-82-7   9.95

PASSION'S LEGACY by Lori Paige. 224 pp. Sarah is swept into
the arms of Augusta Pym in this delightful historical romance.
                                        ISBN 0-941483-81-9   8.95

THE PROVIDENCE FILE by Amanda Kyle Williams. 256 pp.
2nd Madison McGuire Mystery.   ISBN 0-941483-92-4   8.95

I LEFT MY HEART by Jaye Maiman. 320 pp. 1st Robin Miller
Mystery.   ISBN 0-941483-72-X   10.95

THE PRICE OF SALT by Patricia Highsmith (writing as Claire
Morgan). 288 pp. Classic lesbian novel, first issued in 1952 . . .
acknowledged by its author under her own, very famous, name.
                                            ISBN 1-56280-003-5   9.95

SIDE BY SIDE by Isabel Miller. 256 pp. From beloved author of
Patience and Sarah.   ISBN 0-941483-77-0   9.95

STAYING POWER: LONG TERM LESBIAN COUPLES by
Susan E. Johnson. 352 pp. Joys of coupledom. ISBN 0-941-483-75-4   14.95

SLICK by Camarin Grae. 304 pp. Exotic, erotic adventure.
                                            ISBN 0-941483-74-6   9.95

NINTH LIFE by Lauren Wright Douglas. 256 pp. 2nd Caitlin
Reece Mystery.   ISBN 0-941483-50-9   8.95

PLAYERS by Robbi Sommers. 192 pp. Sizzling, erotic novel.
                                            ISBN 0-941483-73-8   9.95

MURDER AT RED ROOK RANCH by Dorothy Tell. 224 pp.
1st Poppy Dillworth Mystery.   ISBN 0-941483-80-0   8.95

LESBIAN SURVIVAL MANUAL by Rhonda Dicksion. 112 pp.
Cartoons!   ISBN 0-941483-71-1   8.95

A ROOM FULL OF WOMEN by Elisabeth Nonas. 256 pp.
Contemporary Lesbian lives.   ISBN 0-941483-69-X   9.95

THEME FOR DIVERSE INSTRUMENTS by Jane Rule. 208 pp.
Powerful romantic lesbian stories.   ISBN 0-941483-63-0   8.95

CLUB 12 by Amanda Kyle Williams. 288 pp. Espionage thriller
featuring a lesbian agent!   ISBN 0-941483-64-9   8.95

DEATH DOWN UNDER by Claire McNab. 240 pp. 3rd Carol
Ashton Mystery.   ISBN 0-941483-39-8   9.95

MONTANA FEATHERS by Penny Hayes. 256 pp. Vivian and
Elizabeth find love in frontier Montana.   ISBN 0-941483-61-4   8.95

LIFESTYLES by Jackie Calhoun. 224 pp. Contemporary Lesbian
lives and loves.   ISBN 0-941483-57-6   9.95

WILDERNESS TREK by Dorothy Tell. 192 pp. Six women on
vacation learning ''new'' skills.   ISBN 0-941483-60-6   8.95

MURDER BY THE BOOK by Pat Welch. 256 pp. 1st Helen
Black Mystery.   ISBN 0-941483-59-2   9.95

These are just a few of the many Naiad Press titles — we are the oldest and
largest lesbian/feminist publishing company in the world. Please request a
complete catalog. We offer personal service; we encourage and welcome
direct mail orders from individuals who have limited access to bookstores
carrying our publications.